Hetaira

A Mason Briggs Mission

Annette Goeres

This is a work of complete and utter fiction.
Any resemblance to reality is a huge coincidence

To M.M. (you know why) and B.G., as usual.
Couldn't have done it without you

Prologue

Porter was nervous. It had finally come. All his dodging and rationalizing was about to be destroyed.

"You ready?" Mason asked from behind him. Porter turned, noting his friend's slight smile.

"I suppose. I've never done this before. I guess I am nervous." He straightened his tie unnecessarily.

Mason's smile widened. "Uh, yeah, you know Catholics really aren't supposed to have lots of experience getting married a lot."

"Shut up." Porter said absently.

Mason laughed. "Here. Give me the ring now, before you fucking drop it."

Porter smiled back ruefully. "You're right. My hands are not very steady, are they?"

"No, you look like a fucking leaf caught in a tornado."

"It's not that fucking bad."

Mason snorted. "Whatever, man. You believe whatever you like. Just give me the ring."

Porter sighed. This promised to be moderately unpleasant. He had never been into weddings anyway. He had certainly never considered that he might someday actually get married. "Here. Try not to fucking lose it." He handed over the ring and then raked through his dark curls distractedly.

Mason laughed. "You try not to fucking lose it!"

Porter also laughed. "Watch me fucking lose it and run!"

"You better not! Michael will tackle you halfway down the aisle and bring you back."

"He would love that, wouldn't he?"

"You would deserve it, too."

"Yeah, yeah, whatever."

They turned to go into the main church. Mason glanced at Porter quickly. "Just a second, man. Your boutonniere is a bit off."

Porter took a deep breath and closed his eyes while Mason

reached up and fiddled with the stupid flowers. "Done?"

"Yeah, you look sort of presentable now. If you weren't so damn tall, it wouldn't matter so much, you freak. No one would see them if you weren't towering over us all."

"Fuck you."

"Oh, I don't know, Porter." Mason said with a very sly look. "I think that is your department. Later, that is."

Porter blushed furiously. Then he smiled. "Of course. I am fucking nervous about that, too!"

Mason nodded seriously. "You'll be just fine. Just treat her like the lady we all know she is."

"Of course."

Mason bowed and gestured Porter to walk in front of him.

Father Greg had the same amused smile on his face that Mason had. Porter noted it and sighed. Oh well. At least all his friends were going to enjoy this. Nervously, he straightened his tie again.

"Peace, my son." Father Greg said softly.

"Oh, I am trying, Father; I am trying."

Juan, Gabriella, Michael, Karen, James and Callie were in the pews. Porter didn't want too many people at his wedding anyway. Close friends mattered far more to him than numbers.

While they waited for Sienna to show up, Mason whispered, "When are you getting back?"

"James and I have to fly into Tangier right after we wrap here for a buying contact. Callie and Sienna get to go along, lucky girls."

Mason snorted softly. "They are stuck on a plane with you for how many hours? They are not lucky, believe me."

"Shut up."

The doors at the back of the church opened. Miguel had been taking pictures the whole time and he positioned himself to get some good shots of Sienna.

She was glowing, of course. She was always radiant to Porter. Her white dress was simple, and she held a single lily. There was short veil in her light brown hair. That was about all Porter could remember later.

The ceremony was very simple, and there was a small brunch afterwards, since it was only 10:30 in the morning. As everyone chatted and laughed together, Mason leaned over to Porter. "You and James are buying then?"

"Yes, we need to increase inventory. It is a quick trip. This is a man we've done business with here, and he wants to fete us there. Could be a great contact for us."

"You know there has been unrest in that area, right?"

Porter nodded. "Yes, but I do not think it will reach Tangier. It is mostly in the Sahara region."

"You're probably right."

James, his blond hair catching the sunlight, leaned over. "You know we only have about an hour before we need to leave, right, sir?"

Porter sighed. "James, use my fucking name, please. And yes, I know."

James nodded. "Of course, Porter. You know it is awkward for me still."

"You are a partner, not a servant."

"It is still awkward. Anyway, I just wanted to make sure you were aware of the time."

"Yes, thank you."

Mason looked distracted still. Porter knew him pretty well, so he waited. Mason focused back on him soon enough. "Look, I am a bit worried. If you have trouble, or something happens that makes you nervous, let me know. I will do what I can."

Porter nodded. "I will, Mason. Now let's forget that shit and have some fun for a while yet."

Mason laughed and raised his glass.

An hour later, Porter, Sienna, James and the red-headed Callie were bidding their friends goodbye and leaving for the airport. Mason was driving them.

"Thanks, Mason." Porter said as he got out and handed suitcases to James.

"It is no problem, Porter. Just remember what I said. Something is bugging me, and I am not fucking sure what."

Porter looked at Mason for a long moment. "I will remember. If you think of what it was, let me know. I trust your intuition."

"Good. Have fun."

"See you later."

The flight was uneventful, although Porter was bothered by Mason's warning. It was vague, but Mason was often right about things like that. He had access to lots of information that Porter didn't have, and he certainly could have zeroed in on something. Even if he couldn't pinpoint exactly what it was, Porter didn't want to ignore it. Mason was too smart for Porter to ignore. Mason joked that Porter was brilliant, but Porter knew he wasn't the leader Mason was. He might have been smart and clever; Mason was the one they all trusted with very good reason.

"My dear, did you hear me at all?" Sienna asked, bringing him out of his distracted musing.

"What? Oh, no, I am afraid I did not."

"I know. I asked what you were thinking about?"

"Mason wanted us to be careful. There has been an increase in militia activity in Morocco recently, mostly in the southwest."

"Ah, I see."

Porter shrugged. "Forewarned is forearmed, my dear."

"Of course."

"It is bugging me more than I would like. Let's just be careful, all of us."

"Yes, Porter, of course. Would you like to talk more?"

"No, at least, not about that. We can discuss other things instead."

Sienna smiled a wicked smile. "I can think of several things we should absolutely not discuss in mixed company."

"Not what I meant, Sienna."

She laughed.

They were met at the airport in Tangier by Mahmoud Abdul, the diamond seller they had come to see. He was an outstanding host and Porter began to relax some. He hated flying anyway. Mason's warning hadn't helped much. Porter made a mental note to slap Mason upside the head for it when they got back. Fucking serve him right.

Once they were in the diamond broker's office, the negotiations began in earnest. Porter and James were good judges of what they wanted, and Mahmoud was not out to gouge them. Porter found himself nervously playing with his new wedding band. That was going to take some getting used to.

As they wound down the negotiations, there was a knock at the door. Mahmoud looked irritated. "I wanted no interruption!" He said loudly.

Someone answered through the door but the words were indistinct.

Mahmoud shook his head. "I beg your pardon, gentlemen and ladies. I am most distressed by this. Pray excuse me." He stood and strode to the door.

"Of course, Mr. Abdul." Porter murmured.

Mahmoud opened the door. "I thought I left clear orders that..." He never finished the sentence. There was the crack of at least two rifles and Mahmoud reeled back.

He knew what the sound was before he even thought it all the way through. Porter found he had instinctively thrown himself out of his chair at the gunshots and had knocked both Sienna and Callie to the floor. He covered them, James behind him. As he crouched over the women, Porter noted that Mahmoud was dead. He had a neat bullet hole right through his forehead and another red splotch on his chest. Four men stormed the room, shouting to other people outside. Porter didn't really register what they were saying. He couldn't get his brain to move fast enough to take in more than random details.

He had retreated to the part of his mind that deliberately ignored emotional involvement. It was the part of him that was the most logical, and would help the most in this situation, he knew. He watched in the same detached manner as the four men checked Mahmoud. They trained the automatic rifles on the buyers on the floor, still talking to each other.

Porter noticed that they all had head coverings on, the traditional keffiyeh that were worn by the Islamic groups in the area. It didn't mean much beyond the fact that those scarves provided convenient disguises. Anyone could wear one. Porter didn't put much weight on it. The men also had scarves over their lower faces. He wouldn't be able to positively identify any of them.

"Get up!" One of them barked in the accented English they were using. He gestured violently with his rifle. Porter carefully put his hands behind his head and stood slowly. James, Sienna and Callie also stood slowly.

The men in the room looked them over. One of them shouted out to the hall, "You get in here. You will be wanting this."

Another man nodded vigorously. "Yes, you will want indeed."

Porter didn't think. He somehow knew he should only observe for now. Another man, without the face cover, came in. He had swarthy skin and finely-chiseled features. Porter would be able to pick him out if he ever got the chance. The leader, as he appeared to be, looked at them for a minute. Then he smiled slowly. "Yes, I think so. Take the women. Dispose of the men."

"But, sir!"

He held up a hand imperiously. "No, listen. Think of the international outcry when we take these. Even if there is none, we will sell them the same as the others. They will bring a premium anyway." Two men grabbed Sienna. She struggled some, but Porter knew she wasn't trying too hard. She was worried about the rifles still trained on James and himself. Callie looked simply terrified. If they got out of this shithole, Porter would have to give her some instructions on how to fight. If they lived. Of course, right now he was going to have to figure out a way to live, period. To hell with fighting.

Sienna was still struggling when the men shot them. She

screamed, overcome by the events that were taking place. Porter tried to move out of the way even as he knew it was hopeless. There was no way to move that fast. It was an instinctive, stupid, punitive thing. Even if they missed somehow, there were enough backups around to make sure of a follow up. He felt a hot burning low in his left side. Then he felt warm blood pouring down. Sudden weakness overcame him. He hated weakness, fought it with all his training, but gravity was simply too strong for him. The ground seemed very soft for some reason. Porter rolled to his side agonizingly slowly and looked at Sienna dimly. If he was going to die, he at least wanted to see her for the last time. Too bad he didn't have the energy to make a lovely death-speech like the movies always seemed to have. Fucking inconsiderate of reality. Sienna looked as beautiful as she always did. It was a good way to die.

The shot had taken him too low to kill him outright but he was losing blood fast. He still might die from that. Fuck. He thought dying on his wedding day should take some fucking years off his stint in Purgatory.

Sienna managed to throw the men trying to force her out the door off and ran to him. The shot had gone wide and he was hit in the side only. He was too smart to try and stop them, not that he could do anything anyway. Not when he was this fucking weak.

Sienna gently turned him all the way over, still faking hysteria. She checked him quickly. Porter noted incuriously that she was trying to get her rings off, but her hands were too slippery with his blood. James was also still alive, although it might end up a close thing if they didn't get attention soon. Porter saw him breathing.

He carefully winked at Sienna. Someone wretched her upright, and this time she allowed herself to be pulled away. The other men didn't finish the job. Porter thought they might have lost their stomach for shooting when they saw it up close and calculated.

"What do you think the Army of the Almighty will do if this does get out?" One of them asked, casually leaning against the desk.

One of the others snorted from where he was raiding the safe. "Whatever Emil the Madman wants, as we always have! He is right. We *shall be infamous for this."*

" That is what Emil wants. These are finished, or will be soon."

They all left. Porter made sure he could not hear or feel any footsteps before he rolled over again. Fuck, he was hit hard. Carefully he pressed a handkerchief to his side and crawled to check James. He'd be okay. In fact, he was probably better off than Porter. The bullet had ricocheted off his card case and had only gone through skin.

Porter groaned aloud as he forced himself to stand and leaned shakily against the desk. Fuck. This was going to be a mess.

"Lord Jesus Christ, have mercy on me a sinner." He whispered as he fumbled around in his pocket and pulled out his cell phone. Better call this one in now, while he was still conscious. Mason would have to be on it as soon as possible. He needed fucking help, and only Mason could do this. Porter called Mason's number even as he sank to the floor again, leaning heavily against the desk and trembling.

He only prayed that Mason wasn't somewhere with his phone turned off.

Part I

Chapter 1

"So, what do you suppose they're doing?" Juan asked casually, playing with his wine glass. They had all adjourned to Mason's house after the reception and had been there for several hours. Good friends like hanging out together with very little incentive.

Mason glanced at his watch. "Probably still buying, Johnny. This is Porter and James; not to say that they are all anal-retentive or anything, but they are anal-retentive and shit."

Juan laughed. "So true!"

Gabriella sighed. "It was a nice wedding, too. I like weddings. They give me so many ideas. Might be useful later on." She smiled wickedly at Juan, who promptly choked on his wine. Her cocoa skin was beautifully highlighted by her red dress.

"I'll just bet they do." Mason smiled.

"Maybe, when I get married, I'll be able to walk on my own down the aisle. That'd be fucking awesome." She gestured vaguely at the carved cane she relied on to help her balance still. Mason noticed she had grown her black hair out quite a bit since last time she'd had it down.

"That's hardly necessary, Gabriella." Juan said gently.

She shrugged. "I know, but it would be nice all the same."

Karen also nodded. "I understand." She also looked stunning in an ivory column gown. Michael had obviously been completely distracted during the car ride. Come to think on it, he still seemed distracted anytime she stood up. Served him right, Mason thought. Michael was so used to being in charge of any situation just by sheer physical mass.

Mason's phone buzzed in his pocket. "Someone's calling. It's probably important then." He sighed, hoping it wasn't a patient or the clinic because he would have to cut short this time with friends. He glanced at the name on his screen. "Oh, it's Porter. Maybe they are done buying now and ready to leave." Everyone became quiet expectantly as he answered his phone. "Hello?"

"Mason, get your fucking ass here. Now. They took her." Porter said abruptly.

15

Mason stood up hurriedly. "What? Slow the fuck down. Who has whom?"

Porter sounded very tense. "Army of the Almighty. They shot Mahmoud, stole his diamonds, took Sienna and Callie and shot us. Mason, get here, please! They fucking took her! Please, Mason! I need you!" His voice started to rise at the end; he was losing control.

"Porter, slow down!" Mason said sharply. This was bad. This was very bad. That goddamn madman had finally gone too far and fucked the wrong people. Mason knew that some line had been crossed. He'd have to do something. But first, he had to calm Porter down. "I can't get there for a little while. Besides, I need some support. How badly are you hurt? And can I put this on speaker phone so everyone can hear?"

"Yeah, whatever, it's probably fucking easier if everyone hears."

Mason put the phone down and turned on the speaker. "Okay, they're all listening. Go."

Porter took a deep, shaky breath on his end. "We were wrapping the deal. Some guys busted in and shot Mahmoud. They seemed a bit surprised that we were there, or maybe it was just that women were there. Anyway, they called in another guy, some leader, I think. They called him Emil the Madman behind his back. Then he said that they were taking the women and to kill James and myself. One guy tried to protest, but Emil said it would make the world take notice, and even if it didn't, they would sell the women at a premium with the others anyway. Then they shot us, and Sienna faked hysteria to make sure we were alive and all, then they pulled them out. And that's all I fucking know. James is still unconscious. He hit his head on the way down. It was about ten minutes ago that they came in."

Mason was thinking rapidly. "You're sure they said the Army of the Almighty?"

"Yes, Mason. I haven't heard of them."

"No, probably not."

Michael slammed his hand into the table. "Fucking hell!"

"Michael!" Mason barked. "Enough!"

16

"No one is fucking doing that! I am going to fucking tearing his ass apart with my bare fucking hands! Bastard!"

"Fucking shut the hell up! Give me some damn time!"

"Unfortunately, we don't have time." Juan said softly. "This will come out, and it will be scandalous on the international scene. That's probably what they want. They can't buy that fucking level of exposure."

"I think so." Porter agreed. "They mentioned that at least Emil wants notoriety."

"Okay, here's what will happen." Mason said. "I have to get in to the Secretary about this. Porter, get yourself somewhere safe. I will send Michael and Juan as soon as I can get a private plane for them."

"I'll fucking fly us both if you can't." Michael growled.

"Michael, you are going to do exactly what I tell you and nothing else. Right now, I cannot have you running off doing your own fucking thing. Either you do it the way I tell you or you can fucking stay behind. Decide, right now." Mason snapped his fingers at Michael. "Now, Michael!"

"Fine, okay, you win, Mason."

"Good. Juan, you better keep a fucking close eye on him. I am counting on you for that. Heavily."

Juan nodded.

"Porter, you and James must be safe. Could you finger these guys?"

"Only Emil. The others had their faces covered."

"Fuck. It'll have to be good enough. Can you get somewhere safe?"

"Shit, Mason, I don't know. I was hit pretty hard. I bet I can't even fucking walk right now. And I can't carry James. I'm too fucking weak. I'm running on straight adrenaline." Porter sounded very dubious.

"Damn! Can you at least lock the door where you are?"

"Uh, yeah, I think so."

"Do it. Don't open it until Michael and Juan are there. The usual code. I have to get this started on this end. And Porter?"

17

"Yeah?"

"Keep it the fuck together until we are there."

"I'll try. I might pass out, though. I have lost a lot."

"Is there water in the room?"

"A little. Not much."

"Stay as hydrated as you can. Michael and Juan are on their way right now. Literally. They just left out the door."

"Good. Mason, thanks. Get here, please."

Mason hung up. "God damn fucking hell!" He said loudly. "Fuck!" He added, for good measure. What the hell was that idiot doing, anyway?

"That sums it up nicely." Gabriella said softly. "Can I do anything?"

"You might have to, Gabriella. And I am sorry for it, because it will put you and Karen into a dangerous situation."

Gabriella shrugged. "It won't be the first, and I want to help. I am just not sure how much I can do with my fucking legs being what they are still."

"We'll just have to see. Let me make two calls, then we will see how this is going to proceed." Mason quickly called an acquaintance that owned a hanger and set up the plane for Michael and Juan. "And now for the hard one." Mason took a deep breath, let it out slowly, and called a top secret number.

"Six-eight-seven-seven-naught-four." The voice on the other end said softly.

"Four-three-nine-seven-five-one." Mason responded.

"This had better be important, Dr. Briggs." The Secretary growled.

"Oh, it is. You see, two of my associates, American citizens, were just grabbed by the Army of the Almighty in Tangier and the Army shot two other American citizens. If you let me handle it, I will do it quietly. If you don't, it is going to blow up and there will be lots of pressure on the administration to do something, and soon."

"You're sure about this information?" The Secretary asked sharply.

"Absolutely."

"Damn it, what are they thinking?"

"I believe that they wish to be taken seriously by the international community as a militia. Also, it is being led by Emil."

"That man is still in charge? He's insane!"

"I know. And yes, my associate actually saw and can identify him."

"What else is that mad man doing?"

"Auctioning the American women he's grabbed."

"What? When?"

"You heard me. The two he has taken are to be auctioned, probably at the slave pens in a few days."

"This is possibly the worst timing he could have hit on."

"I know. So which is it? You going to give it to me and give me information and support, or is there going to be military action?"

"I can't make that decision!"

"No, but you need to talk to the president right now and find out. I will go in, either with your help, or I can do it publically."

"All right, Doctor. Please hold off until I can get official orders from the president."

"You can have two hours. After that, I have to start calling journalists. I will go after my team."

"I understand." The Secretary hung up.

"Fuck." Mason said softly. This day just turned from beautiful to shit in about fifteen minutes. He put his face in his hands, thinking rapidly still. He needed to get ready to go, pretty much now. He was betting the president wouldn't want to move. The war hawks would be all over this, and the politically peaceful would raise hell. He was sure the administration would want it handled as quietly as possible. "Ladies," he said, his face still covered. "Get some clothes together, for you and the men, as well as Porter and James. We're going to be leaving soon and I

19

need you ready as soon as you can be. We have to get out of here within an hour, maybe less."

They left without comment. Mason didn't look up. This was one hell of a mess now. Finally, he sighed and began to clear his table. That idiot had finally grabbed the wrong people. It had only been a matter of time before he tried it once too often. This was it. Grimly, Mason started his dishwasher and went to collect clothes and other items he might need. Shit was going down. It would go down hard. It was time that the bastard got what he really deserved, and Mason was going to serve it up as quickly as he could. Revenge definitely was not best served cold.

Chapter 2

The phone rang. It was Juan. "Hey, Mason, bring me any electronics you have. I grabbed my basic component kit, but it might be a bit hard to get stuff ready on the fly. I don't know what your plan is, but we might need the support. Also, grab my laptop and a 3D printer. We might need those."

"All right, Juan. Anything else you need?"

"Yeah, Michael wants you get him some clothes. You know how hard it is to get shit that fits the big gorilla."

In the background, Mason heard Michael say, "Shut the fuck up, Juan. I am gonna get you for that." It made Mason smile to hear, so he appreciated it.

"I will, Juan, but when we are there, we are going to be disguised as part of the Army of the Almighty. You won't need much with your skin and eyes already, but Michael is going dark. I will bring the clothes. Robes and the like so I shouldn't need to bring anything else."

"Ah, you do have a plan, then. Good. I hate trying to fuck people over without a plan. Where we headed once we land?"

"The diamond trader's name was Mahmoud Abdul. You'll be able to locate him. Porter will only open the door with the right code, so make sure you get it right or he might plant a knife between your eyes for you."

"He doesn't have his knives on him."

Mason snorted. "As if that makes any fucking difference. He'll improvise something if he has to. You know he's made use of a letter opener before, messily. Just make sure Michael knows. I don't want those two having a fight. That could end badly and they would both hate it."

"No, I agree with that assessment. And the girls?"

"They are coming with me. I need someone in there who can be in the main pens. They are probably going to segregate Sienna and Callie. Gabriella and Karen are going to be smuggled in."

"All right, Mason. I trust you on this. We are getting ready to take off now. Work it out and be ready when we land. I want this shit over and done, for good. If I see that fucking moron, I am going to blow his fucking head off. I'm just giving you fair warning."

"No, you're not."

Juan laughed. "No, you're right there. I am not. Michael will do it for me."

"No, you're not! Neither of you will do anything."

"Yeah, chill, Mason. We know. Hasta."

Mason shook his head as he ended the call. Juan was good, but he was impulsive. The plan that Mason was working with meant Juan was going to have to curb that. It was the short notice that was going to be hard for them all. Oh well. The fucking idiot in Morocco had dictated the timeline. Now Mason would have to respond.

His phone rang again. "Hello?"

"Dr. Briggs?" It was the Secretary. Mason sat up expectantly.

"Yes, speaking."

"You have the go-ahead. However, the president wants it as quiet as you can handle it. I know you are the soul of discretion, but I was told to stress that there can be no international attention on this matter until after it has been taken care of. The administration cannot be involved in Morocco at this time. We are engaged in high-level talks with all the Islamic states right now, and we can't be embarrassed by something coming out. At least, not in the open. If you are successful, be sure to let me know. It could be useful in the talks."

"I understand. It would aid my team if I had access to certain technology."

"Whatever you need, Doctor. What do you need and when?"

"I need some top-quality skin dye and hair coloring. I also require some small electronic bugs, and some loose components. And I need some disguises. I leave within the hour. I need it all by then."

There was a slight pause. Mason knew he was pushing this. He needed the stuff now or else it would have to be left; time was as necessary as people right now. Finally, the Secretary said, "All right. I will have it at the airport in the hanger with the jet you're taking."

Mason didn't ask how the Secretary knew where they were leaving from. "Thank you, Sir. I am sorry to have to push on this."

"I understand, Dr. Briggs. It is possible that you would have been asked to take on this army anyway, you know."

"I figured. Well, I have a jet to catch. I will talk to you on completion of this mission, Sir."

"Good luck."

Mason ran over the list of his stuff mentally as he surveyed what he had out on his bed. This had to be finished within three days. Any longer would be too dangerous. The slave sales would be then. There was no way to keep Emil from spreading his own shit around, so there would be ample interest in this sale in particular. The Madman would want Sienna and Callie to bring in premium prices, and he would be counting on international attraction. Mason was also counting on the heightened interest now. There had to be lots of potential buyers who might be new to the situation. They could insinuate themselves more easily that way.

He scooped all the stuff on his bed into a travel suitcase. He made sure Ninja's cat food was full and that there was ample water for his pet then locked his house and drove to get Gabriella and Karen. They would be going with him. He needed the ears they would provide.

"All right, ladies. Here is how this is going to have to work: Juan and Michael are going to infiltrate as guards. You two are going to end up smuggled into the slave pens. This idiot has been amassing women and men to sell for about a month now. He wants to get money and show he is serious. Unstable though he is, he's still very shrewd. Anyway, I need you two to be in on it."

Karen looked scared but she nodded. "Understood, Mason. We will do it, right, Gabriella?"

Gabriella also nodded.

Mason glanced at her cane. "You won't be able to take that in. How much can you walk without it?"

"Enough, Mason. Just don't expect me to win any races."

23

Mason nodded. "We'll have to alter your skin a bit, Karen. And your hair. But the good news is that you will mostly be wearing a burqua. It'll be hot as hell, but you will be as anonymous as you can be."

They both nodded. Mason was silent as he thought and drove. This was going to be a hell of a job to pull, and it had to be fast. The sale would be in days. They had to be ready and moving in Morocco by tomorrow.

The private jet was fueled and waiting for them. Mason recognized the pilot and co-pilot. At least the government was on top of that. The pilot shook his hand and said, "There are several bags for you in the hold."

"Excellent. We won't keep you waiting, then. Let's get this show going."

"Sir!"

Mason sat and put on his seat belt. Then he sent a text to Juan. It merely said, "Leaving." Juan would know what to do with it, once he and Michael landed. They would be ahead of their own jet by about an hour and a half unless Michael had shaved time by flying a pattern that was through restricted space. Mason hoped not. He didn't want to try and undo that sort of incident along with the mess he already had.

Karen looked worriedly out the window as their jet began to taxi for takeoff. "Do you think they are okay?" She asked.

Mason figured she probably wasn't referring to Porter and James. "Unless Michael gets excited, yes."

She smiled slightly, still looking worried. "He does that, doesn't he?"

Gabriella gently patted her arm. "Juan will keep him calm. If nothing else, he will tell jokes non-stop until Michael listens."

Karen laughed. "So true!" She sighed then. "Sometimes, I wish I was the one he depended on more."

Gabriella nodded. "I understand, but look at it this way: you are way better looking than Juan is. You can't monopolize everything!"

Karen laughed again and the jet began to pick up speed.

Gabriella winked at Mason. He smiled at her. She had the read of the situation right.

"By the way, Gabriella," Mason said as they took off. "How are your legs, really?"

Gabriella sighed. "I still have balance issues. Who knew that toes were that important, anyway? And the scars are rather dreadful-looking, but the muscles have all healed well. I can walk and all, I just shuffle. And I tend to overbalance if I am not concentrating." She looked down disconsolately at her legs. "Sometimes, I admit that I wish the bomb had gone off just a smidgeon sooner. Then I would be dead."

"That's probably normal, you realize." Mason said gently.

"Shit, I hope so."

"Are you still seeing Dr. Curtis?"

"Yes, but less. Once a month."

"Who's Dr. Curtis?" Karen asked.

"One of the doctors in my office." Mason replied.

"Oh." Karen quickly looked back out her window.

Gabriella smiled. "Karen, I am not ashamed that I need psychological help. I still am having real problems accepting that I am no longer whole and that I cannot have babies. Because, let's be honest about it, Juan would be a wonderful father, and his children would be gorgeous. Come on, don't you think the same things about Michael?"

Karen blushed slowly. "Um, I hadn't really thought about it before. Not really."

"Well, don't you want to have sex with him?"

Karen blushed harder. "I don't really know." She mumbled. "Sex has always been such a, I don't know, possessive thing before. Like a power play or something."

Gabriella shrugged. Mason sighed. "It was used as a power play against you, Karen. Sex is not supposed to be a dominating or violent thing. It is supposed to be an expression of love, not a weapon of lust." Karen nodded, but Mason was pretty sure she didn't believe him. "Give it time. I am fairly sure Michael will persuade you, eventually."

Gabriella glanced at Mason. "What are the chances that we will be in the danger of something like that where we are going, Mason?"

"It shouldn't happen. For one thing, Juan and Michael will be there. But the biggest reason is that Emil holds to a very strange, hard-line reading of the Qur'an. He explicitly forbids his men to touch women at all, if it can be avoided. Not sure how that is going to work, if he wants new followers, but that is how he holds right now. I think it is one of those fanatical misogynist failings of his. The unfortunate part is that he has power, but at least you should be safe. Make no mistake, my dears, he intends to sell the women he has captured. He intends to break apart marriages to make his own grip stronger. He wants to sell the men separately, and he wants them to go to different places. His followers tend to be unmarried young men, so they don't see this as something wrong, only as something politically expedient. He has done it before, and I think he intends to do it again."

Mason leaned forward, making sure he had both their attention. "He separates the women into virgins and not, and virgins claim a much higher price. He has Sienna and Callie, both very desirable women anyway, and he will want to showcase them. Just because you aren't virgins doesn't make you lesser, all right? I need you two more than I need them, to be honest. I must have the women in those pens aware of what we are doing. They will be the key. They can turn this all. You two have to win them over, do you understand?"

Gabriella and Karen stared at him for quite a while. Mason knew he could have broken it to them differently; however he needed them to sense the urgency for what he needed from them, and that required less finesse than he had time for. Finally, Karen nodded. "All right, Mason. I will do it. Just make sure you can get us out. I don't want to be part of some guy's harem."

Mason smiled slightly. "No, no harem could ever contain you, either of you. Michael is one hell of a lucky guy, to have someone as strong as you."

Karen flushed again. "I'm not strong." She whispered, staring out the window again. "Especially not compared to Michael."

"Whatever, Karen. I don't see him volunteering to be in a place as scary as a slave pen. And I don't hear him saying he will do what you are saying you will do."

Karen shook her head stubbornly. Mason sighed again. She wasn't ready yet. He wasn't sure how much longer she could put off the truth before it started to affect her.

Gabriella seemed to think the same, because she reached over and firmly turned Karen back towards them. "Look, girl, I know you have had a hard go of it. But Mason doesn't lie about shit like this. Neither do I. Don't call me a liar. I see a beautiful and strong young woman who is going to kick an idiot's ass and hand it to him on a platter. Now, Michael can certainly kick ass, but he won't be able to convince people to follow him. You will, you are, and this Emil guy is going to fucking wish he had never heard of the Army of the Almighty because of you, and only you." Karen started to say something, but Gabriella held up her hand. "No, I am not listening to any protests. You are going to kick ass. You are kick-ass. The end."

Karen smiled in spite of herself. "Okay, okay!"

"That's better. Start accepting that you are worthy of him, and the rest will fall into place, including the sex."

Karen smiled still as she shrugged. "I guess I have to. You don't leave me any choices."

"I know." Gabriella shrugged. "I am sorry that I had to be blunt. Sometimes that is the best way."

"No apology is needed, my dear. Let's feed this moron his own plan."

"That's my girl."

Chapter 3

The landing was uneventful and before the airplane was finished taxiing, Mason had called Juan.

"Hello?" Juan answered right away.

"We're here. How is everything?"

"Well, Porter was pretty close to passing out again by the time we got here. Michael wanted to take a shortcut or seven but I talked him out of it."

"Good."

"Yeah, he's pretty fucking pissed with me still."

"Then Porter must have passed out before?"

"At least once, from what he said."

"Fuck, that's bad. He must have been hit hard."

"Well, I am no doctor, unlike some people I could name, but he bled a lot. The bullet didn't hit anything vital, but it went through. I think he had a bit of trouble getting both entry and exit covered." Mason started swearing. "Let me know when you run out of words, Mason. I have an excellent command of swearing and I am pretty good at making shit up."

"All right, where the fuck are you guys?"

"Still here, in Mahmoud's place. Porter passed out finally and we didn't want to try moving the old pirate without you. James is fine, but he's really shaken up. I think he is pissed as hell, too, but I am not sure. He hasn't said anything since he woke up according to Porter."

"Nothing?"

"Nope."

"Fuck! This just gets better all the fucking time! Stay there; we're coming right now."

"Get here soon, Mason." Juan said seriously. "I might not be able to keep this contained much longer. Porter is gonna be fucking pissed and Michael is getting more pissed by the minute. He's gonna start something soon if you don't give us direction. Just make sure he has Karen to give him someone to look after."

Mason hung up. He looked at the sky. "Little fucking help, God?"

A taxi had pulled up to take them to the diamond seller's business. Gabriella and Karen were looking carefully at Mason for instruction. The trouble was he was not sure what to expect exactly. Fuck!

"Let's go." He said shortly. The cab driver quickly helped load the bags and they were at the office in short order. Mason had requested the attack be hushed in the news. There were two discreet soldiers standing outside. That was all. They stood aside after a glance towards the cabman.

The interior of the business office looked awful. Papers were strewn all over, desks and chairs thrown around, cabinets hung open and empty.

"Holy shit." Gabriella said softly as she looked around.

"Yeah." Karen agreed. She quickly began clearing a path on the floor. "Here, Gabriella. Don't trip."

"Thank you." Gabriella said, making her slow way after Karen. She was hampered without the cane but not incapacitated.

Mason knocked on the door of the office twice, waited two seconds and knocked three times more. There were four staccato knocks from the other side and Juan opened the door. Mason glanced in. "Juan, you and Michael better take James and the ladies to another room. They don't need to see this."

Michael stood up. "Thank you, Mason."

"I'll call if I need your help."

Michael nodded. He and Juan helped James and they quietly exited. Mason didn't need to confirm that Mahmoud was dead; that was pretty obvious. He crossed to Porter.

Porter was still unconscious. Mason noted that his shirt was soaked in blood on the left side. Carefully, he looked at the wounds. Juan and Michael had done a good job and he didn't think there would be any complications. The blood loss was another concern. If he had lost too much, Porter would be too weak to be a major part of Mason's plans. He would have to wake him up to find out.

That proved unexpectedly easy. The fact that Porter did not awaken slowly also complicated things. Mason was fervently glad that Porter didn't have his knives on him. It would have been much worse for Mason.

"Porter!" He said sharply, wrestling with his friend, "Calm down; it's Mason, you ass!"

"Fuck that!" Porter shouted back, still struggling.

"No, man, it's Mason! Chill, man, chill!" Porter started to calm a bit. Mason breathed more easily. The last time he had tussled with Porter, he'd ended up very close to a broken sternum. "Shit, man, you scared me."

"Yeah, sorry." Porter forced himself into a sitting position against the desk. "I guess I thought you were someone else."

"Clearly. How are you, otherwise?"

"Fucking weak. Pissed. The usual."

"Can you walk? We need to get out of here."

"Probably not by myself."

"Then I will help you. Come on."

"Why not Michael? He's better at it." Porter said, wincing as he stood up and leaning against the desk for support.

"Because I think he is going to want to carry Gabriella. She is way prettier than you anyway."

"He would go for the cushy job with benefits." Porter sighed.

Mason was privately glad that Porter was willing to joke about things. He was functioning on at a normal level then. He helped Porter to the door.

"How are you, really?"

Porter's face grew hard. "I'm fucking pissed as hell, what did you fucking think?"

"I was still talking physically, you ass."

"Oh. I think I will be all right, once I get enough water and some food unless you need me in fighting form. You're fucked if that is the case."

"No, no fighting form yet." Mason assured him. They staggered to the door. Porter was significantly taller than Mason, who was six feet himself. "Why are you so fucking tall? Makes things that much harder."

"Because God wanted to humble us both." Porter said, his face paler than usual with the strain. "Now shut the fuck up so I can concentrate."

Once they were out in the hall, Mason shouted, "Juan, Michael, we need to blow this joint and fast." They came out of the conference room down the hall. "Michael, carry Gabriella. We don't have time to be nice."

"Gotcha, Mason."

"Now just a damn minute!" Gabriella started in. Mason glared at her furiously.

"We don't have the fucking time. He's going to carry you and if you want, you can kick and scream the whole damn way. Up to you."

"I can fucking walk."

"You can fucking shut up. I don't have time for this. We gotta get. James, are you all right?"

"Yes." Porter's assistant said softly.

"Are you sure? If you are going to be trouble, I will leave you here."

"No, you won't. I need to get her back."

"Then you need to fucking communicate with us. None of this turtle-shell shit."

"I understand, Mason."

"Good. Let's go."

Chapter 4

Once they had piled into the spacious cab again, Porter leaned his head back on the seat and closed his eyes. Mason was sure the strain he had put himself through was quite high.

"Michael, do you have some water on you?"

"Always." Michael pulled out a small water bottle and handed it to Mason.

"Good. Porter, drink it. Do you need help?" Mason asked as he poured some energy mix into the bottle and shook it to dissolve it.

Porter sighed and sat up wearily again. "I might."

Mason suddenly grinned roguishly. "Here, Karen, you can feed him."

She smiled. Porter sighed again. "What the fuck is the deal with you, Mason?"

"I don't want you to bite me is all." Mason said, still grinning.

"Whatever, man. You have a fucking warped sense of humor."

"It comes from the company I keep, for sure."

Porter drank all the water. "Can I fucking sleep now?" He demanded. Even though he had kept his tone light for all this, Mason knew he needed to rest and reconcile himself to what had happened.

"Sure, Porter. But we are going to talk, you and I are, once we get to our destination."

"Can't wait. Way to fucking ruin a good nap, Mason."

"You're welcome."

Porter winced and leaned back again. "Wasn't a fucking compliment, ass."

Mason shrugged. "It doesn't matter." He glanced at Porter. "Now go to sleep, Porter." He said gently. "We're here." He wasn't sure Porter had heard him, but he gave a soft sigh and seemed to fall asleep.

Juan shook his head. "This is fucked up, Mason."

"I know. So here's what we're going to do. Porter and James are going to stay with me. Juan and Michael, you are going to infiltrate the kitchen staff. You will have more mobility that way. I think I have a way to get Gabriella and Karen into the slave pen. It will depend on some things you two will verify for me. The three of us will work from our end as new buyers. We'll have heard about these new women, and we might be interested. However, to reduce any problems we might run into, I will be the main buyer. Porter and James are going to be assistants or slaves, whichever is in vogue currently. The first thing that is going to happen is everyone except Juan and Gabriella are going to get a lot darker, both hair and skin. I have all the stuff here. Any questions?"

"Not right now. I might need some time to build anything we need though."

"We don't have time. The sale is in…" Mason glanced at his watch to make sure of the date. "Two days now."

"Fuck, that is going to be a tough push, especially if Porter is this weak. He might not be up to it."

"I know that. But you want to tell him?"

"Mason, I may be an incurable optimist but I am not stupid."

"Exactly. And I am not any stupider than you. At least, not on this. I need you and Michael to get in there and get info as soon as possible. You're going in tonight. The night guards are always less observant. James, did the guards use English?"

James nodded. "Yes, Mason. They all had accents, but the accents didn't agree completely."

"That's what I thought. The thing is, he's pulled extremists from many different sectors, and they don't have a common language except English. You two should be good. Once we get to the city we're going towards, we will get Michael all darker and you two can start."

Michael nodded. "Okay, Mason."

"Then, once you get back to me, we'll figure out how to sneak in Karen and Gabriella. I need them in the pens with the other women. They'll be the key to this whole fucking mess."

"What?" Michael looked upset.

"You fucking heard me, Michael. They are going to make sure those other ladies are onto us. We have to have them or this goes to Hell faster than shit."

"That's asking a fucking lot, Mason."

"You think I don't fucking know that?" Mason was too tired to be nice. It was a problem. Michael needed special handling on this type of thing, and Mason had overlooked it. Shit. He still felt like he had to protect everyone all the fucking time.

Karen gently laid her hand on Michael's arm. "We can talk about it privately when we get there, my dear. Let's not have a huge argument here in front of everyone."

Michael shrugged abruptly. He didn't say anything more on the subject though.

Gabriella looked at Juan, her eyebrow raised slightly. "Wanna start something too, Juan?"

Juan grinned back cheekily. "You can make your own fucking decisions."

"Good." Gabriella looked back at Mason. "I am ready, so long as you can give me some coaching."

"Of course. We'll do it there while I get you ladies looking right."

The taxi ride didn't take much longer. Mason brooded the whole time. He hated going into a situation blind but at least this time they knew they were blind. Just made it fucking harder than it should be.

The safe house looked less-than-safe. It blended in well with the neighborhood and would be easy enough to locate, since it was the only one with a green door anywhere for several streets.

"All right, Michael, you and Karen can go work out your differences in the back room." Mason said shortly. He really didn't have time to be gentle and sensitive. This shit had to get resolved soon. "James, go to bed. Now. Don't fucking argue with me. You need to sleep. Porter, wake up; we're here."

Porter's eyes opened immediately. He sat up quickly and winced. "Oh, fuck. I forgot about that." He put his hand to side again. "Damn it, I think it reopened, too."

"You'll be fine, you old pirate. Sometimes I think you are made out of leather and nails." Mason said dispassionately as he helped Porter out of the seat.

"Fuck you." Porter said absently. Mason pulled his arm across his shoulders again. "Mason, I can fucking walk."

"Sure you can. And I can fucking help you, so fucking accept it already."

Porter snorted but subsided. Once inside, he sat at the kitchen table and put his head in his hands. Gabriella and Juan looked a bit warily between Mason and Porter. Juan cleared his throat and said, "We'll go and, uh, have a discussion in a back room."

Mason smiled slightly and nodded.

"What back room?" Gabriella asked, clearly confused.

"Any back room, my dear. Shall we?" Juan was already pulling her out of the room before he'd finished the sentence.

Mason sat at the table across from Porter. "Okay, now that everyone has cleared, we need to talk, Porter. And you know we do."

Porter sighed. He put his hands down on the table and stared at them. "Yes, I know we do." He said very softly.

"I need to know, honestly, if you can help on this or not."

"Honestly? Well, let me think." Porter continued to look at his hands. "Well, once I get some food, I might be better able to tell more honestly."

"Then let's get that taken care of. The government here was most accommodating."

"I just fucking bet."

Mason smiled and got some flat bread out of a cupboard. There was also a crock of yogurt. "Here. Dig in."

"Not too much." Porter dipped the flat bread into the yogurt and ate it slowly. "Got anything to drink?"

"How about water?"

"That'll work, unless you have nothing stronger."

"Porter, this is an Islamic country."

"Oh, I forgot about that. This just gets worse and worse, doesn't it?"

"It'll make it much easier to keep you sick fucks under control."

"Shut the fuck up."

"How are you doing now?"

Porter sighed. "Better, but then again, now it is starting to hit me. I really might need you to talk me out of the black shit I go through, so don't fucking go far."

"Porter, really, I would not put you in danger like that. Have some faith in me, man."

"I do, I do. I promise. I just need the reassurance. I can't go batshit crazy right now."

"No, you may not. There, that should solve that."

Porter smiled faintly. "Yes, mother. Now, what are we going to do?"

"First, we are going to make us all look like we actually belong here. Darker skin, stuff like that. Then Juan and Michael are going to integrate themselves into the guards and Gabriella and Karen are going to be smuggled in with the other women they're going to sell."

"And us?"

"We're going to be buyers, of course. It is usually an auction-type thing, and Emil usually oversees them personally."

"Does he sell men, too?"

Mason shrugged. "Sometimes. Gabriella and Karen are going to rally those women, though. Once they are loose, they are going to turn this."

"Okay, that sounds good." Porter looked around the kitchen. "Is there some fruit or something sweet? I need sugar."

"Here." Mason handed him an apricot spread.

"Hey, this is decent. I could learn to like it."

"We're not going to be here that long."

"When is the sale?"

"You were really out, weren't you? I already said all this in the cab."

"Well, so sorry I was fucking tired."

Mason shook his head mockingly. "Yeah, whatever. The sale is in two days."

"Fuck. I can't see her until then. You'd better make sure of that."

"We could probably arrange it, Porter."

"That would be a terrible idea, Mason. Just trust me on this one. I won't hold my shit together and I might do something fucked and make her lose it, too. We can't chance that."

"Whatever you say. Now, let's make you much darker. Your hair is fine, but your skin is too light. You just can't do anything fucking right, can you?"

Porter smiled again. Mason was relieved that he was able to do that. Maybe it wasn't as bad as that last time Porter lost it.

Chapter 5

Porter's skin took the dye very nicely. He looked curiously in the mirror. "How long will this take to wear off, then?"

"Oh, about a week, I think." Mason said, putting it on his own face and arms. "It'll get lighter and lighter and just go away."

"Good. Your hair is way light now."

"I know. Thank you for pointing out the obvious. I can only do one thing at a time."

"Just trying to help." Porter said in a voice dripping innocence.

"Fuck you, Porter. You are so far beyond helping it isn't even fucking measurable."

"I try." Porter shrugged. "Should we go and tell the others that they can come out of their rooms now?"

"You want to walk into the middle of whatever the hell they are doing? Really?" Mason stared at Porter. "Are you fucking crazy?"

"I suppose that can't be ruled out, but when you put it that way, I think I will stay here and do your hair for you."

Mason laughed. "Very well, darling, just don't take so long this time. Last time was over my break."

"You can't fucking rush genius."

"I bet no hair dresser has ever uttered that particular sentence."

Porter snorted. "I can because I am fucking awesome. Now sit down and shut up."

"You have such a way with words! I bet the ladies all swoon when you say things like that."

"Only the good ones. Do all your hair?"

"You'd better. I don't think highlights are in style here."

"Probably not." Porter was quiet for a few minutes as he combed the dye through Mason's hair. "Care to make a small wager on if Karen and Michael have had the fight out yet and are kissing and making up yet?"

"I would bet that they aren't through the fight yet."

Porter looked at his watch. "We'll find out when they come back.

I note the time and we will just ask."

"Karen will win. Want to wager on that?"

"That's no fucking bet at all, Mason. Betting only makes sense when there is some question about the outcome. Michael will not go down easily though. He has a little trouble accepting that she is her own person still."

Mason shrugged. "We all fail somewhere."

"Except you."

"You are fucking shitting me. I fail all the time."

"Maybe, but not when I need you to fucking succeed."

"We can both fucking pray that this is not the first time then."

Porter sat down at the table. "I am a little shaky on my feet still. Just let me take a breather."

Mason nodded. "Whatever you need. Don't push yourself too hard. You need to function, but you don't need to excel."

"Got it."

Mason watched Porter carefully. "We'll do our best, Porter. You need to help us, but there is always the chance that we won't get them back. You know that, right?"

Porter closed his eyes and his jaw clenched. Then he relaxed slightly. "Yes, I know." He smiled very weakly. "I don't want to hear it though."

"Fuck, Porter, who would? I will try to get you close enough that you can do something to Emil, but what you do is up to you. You don't have to do anything at all."

"Thanks, Mason."

"And I brought you these." Mason passed a small velvet bag to Porter.

Porter took his knives out of the bag carefully. He just looked at them for a few minutes, turning the sheaths over and over in his long fingers. Two tears started from his eyes and he wiped them away quickly. Mason pretended not to notice. "Thanks, Mason. I can't say what this means."

39

"You don't have to say what it means. I am not a total idiot; I knew you would want them. Just be fucking careful. And whatever you do with them, you might end up losing one or two."

"I know. I notice you brought the plain ones."

"Again, Porter, I'm not a total idiot."

"No, not a total idiot at all."

"Hmm, thanks, I think."

"Hey, you set the baseline." Porter pulled the knives from the sheaths and examined them. "All right. I think I am ready then."

"And your ring?"

"I'm not fucking taking it off, Mason." Porter said sharply, putting his right hand over his left protectively.

"I'm not saying you should. I was just asking. Jeez. Bite my fucking head off, idiot."

Porter suddenly grinned. "I fucking worked hard to get the damn thing; I am not taking it off! Fucking what do you take me for, anyway? That damn vow was in front of God and man. You know I can't break vows to God."

"Good. She'll appreciate that. Am I ready then?"

"Well, you're not really my type, but you'll do well enough, I suppose."

Mason shook his head. "I'm glad you are at least able to joke about some things."

"I am, too. I really thought I would be a blubbering ass by now." Porter smiled as he sat back at the table.

"If you need to do that, you can always use another room." Mason invited.

"No, I don't think I do."

"Good. Now you are going to go to bed. You need the sleep. If you refuse, I will give you a sedative. You must heal both your body and your mind."

Porter sighed and put his face in his hands again. "Fine, whatever, Mason. I think we both know I will have nightmares, though. Just… just please don't leave me? I don't think I could handle it if you were gone too. I am so ashamed to say it, but I really need you."

"No, Porter, I won't leave. Juan and Michael are going out tonight. I have to be here. Besides, I have some ladies to coach. I wish you could help with that but you can't. Will you need the shot?"

"Um, well, how about I try it without first, then if I need it I can get it later."

Mason shrugged. "Whatever you want. It needs at least four hours of uninterrupted sleep. Calculate that into your timeline."

"Noted." Porter stood up. He reached across the table and put his hand on Mason's shoulder. "Mason, thanks for coming. I can never pay you back for this."

"You don't ever have to. The fact that I can help you when you need it most is enough."

Porter nodded slightly, tears in his eyes again. Then he drank another bottle of water and went quietly to find the sleeping room James was already in.

Mason slapped his hand on the table in frustration. "Fuck you, Emil! You don't even know what you've done, but you are so fucked now."

Juan came in just then and looked at Mason curiously. "He can't fucking hear you, Mason."

"I don't give a damn, Juan. It makes me feel better to think out loud sometimes."

"I bet that makes your office very entertaining."

Mason smiled. "I don't do it there, ass."

"Oh, damn, that was going to give me incentive to go in. Speaking of which." Juan sat down across from Mason. "How is Porter doing?"

"Better than I hoped."

"Which means what, exactly?"

"He isn't going fucking crazy, for one. Also, he isn't unresponsive. And he seems to be accepting this turn of events, sort of. No one can hope to process it all, of course, but he is not sinking under it. I sent him to try and sleep. He asked me to stay in case he needs help, which, as you know, is a huge fucking step for him."

Juan whistled softly. "Damn, that is good. Relatively speaking."

"Everything's relative, Johnny. How's Gabriella?"

"Napping also. We didn't have anything to argue about, really, so we moved right on to the kissing and making up."

"It's a good way to do things." Mason agreed.

"I did ask her to be as safe as she can, but I can't hold that girl. She won't stand for it. She won't let losing toes hold her back, so who am I to tell her she can't do it?"

Mason sighed. "I hate to throw them into that tiger's den, but we need them."

"I know, Mason. Michael and I will keep them safe. I think that will make the difference."

Mason stood up and got himself a bottle of water. "I sure hope so. Has Karen convinced Michael yet? We really do need you two in there tonight."

"I think she was still working on it when Gabriella fell asleep. It sounded like they were still talking."

"Damn it. I wish that big lunk wasn't so stubborn sometimes."

"It helps him stay focused." Juan shrugged. "Besides, the word is tenacious."

"Stubborn, Juan. He is fucking stubborn as hell. And I fucking need you guys in there. The place has to be cased."

"I know, Mason. I will go hurry it along." Juan stood up. "Just have some food ready to go when I come back so once we have him colored up right we can leave. He'll be hungry."

"What about you? Won't you be hungry?"

"No, Mason. Stress makes me too keyed up to eat. And don't start the fucking lecture." Juan said disgustedly as Mason opened his mouth to protest. "It won't do any fucking good. Not now."

"Fine. I am pissed with you about it though."

"Good. I note the pissed-ness."

42

"That's not even a fucking word."

"Who the fuck cares? Now let me go get the big boy and we can start dying him."

Chapter 6

Juan came back out a minute later. Mason noted he did not bring Michael with him. "Fuck. He isn't ready yet, is he?"

Juan shook his head. "No, and he seems pretty stuck on this."

"Goddamn it. I hate this part."

"You're the best person for it, though, you or Porter. One of you two are sleeping, so it has to be you."

"Thanks for the vote of confidence." Mason said acidly. "How bad is it?"

"Karen was crying."

"Fuck! Well, you better come along as support."

"Good cop/bad cop thing?"

"Sort of, but more like 'mean-ass boss/ nice co-worker'." Mason considered this to be his least favorite job, but Juan was right: he was the best one to do it. He stalked back to the room and slammed the door open. Michael and Karen both spun around to stare at him. "Let's get this done. Our timeline is too tight for me to let you two fucking dance around this anymore. Karen, are you ready and willing to do what I have asked you to do?"

"Yes, Mason, I think I am." Karen said determinedly.

"Just a fucking minute!" Michael protested.

Mason glared at him. "Michael! Is this 1645? Are you married to her? Do you make all her fucking decisions?"

"No, but…"

"Then shut the hell up! I am talking to Karen, not you, right now. She can make her own fucking choices."

"I know, but…"

"No! No 'buts'! Fucking shut up! Now! You cannot ask her to be free and then chain her when she is. Fucking get it through your head that she doesn't need you!" Michael looked angry but he hadn't reacted strongly or taken a swing yet, so Mason figured he was receptive to what he was going to say next. "She doesn't, you ass! Look, she loves you, she likes you, whatever, but she isn't going to stop breathing if you get hurt;

44

she won't die because you do something. That is exactly what I mean. She doesn't need you for her to live. So let her live, fucking moron! Porter didn't die when they stole Sienna, you won't die if she gets grabbed, fucking let it go already!"

"He's right, Mikey." Juan said softly from the doorway. "You know he is. I love Gabriella, but I didn't die when she got hurt. I can't keep her from doing this. She wants to help. I have to let her."

Karen smiled slightly even though she was still crying. "Michael, I like that you want to keep me safe, but you can't keep me safe from my own choices, not when you want me to make them."

Mason took control of the conversation again. "So fucking decide. You can either help, or you can fucking go home. You know I will do it, too. Porter needs you both. You gonna just bitch and moan and fuck around about it from your safe warm house?"

"Mason!" Michael sounded very hurt. "You know I couldn't fucking live with that! How can you even fucking ask me to?"

"Then why are you asking Karen to live with it? Fucking inconsiderate of you."

Michael stood up very straight, looking angry, and opened his mouth to retort, but he stopped, obviously thinking about something. Then he closed his eyes and let a long breath out. "Oh, fuck you, Mason. You are too damn logical. Fucking fuck! Fine, you win. You always do."

"No, Michael, not always. I am trying to help you, too. It isn't just about me winning some stupid argument, you know."

Michael sat down wearily. "God, I fucking hope not. All right, Karen, I guess I have to let you do what you need to. I will try to help where I can."

"Michael," she said simply, "I need to help my friends. It is really important that I show myself that I am able to do that, especially since so many people have helped me."

Michael nodded resignedly. "No, I get it. You do what you need to. Just remember I love you."

"Of course, and I love you."

Juan nudged Mason. "That could've gone worse. We need to get going though."

"I know. Michael, are you going to be okay on this?"

Michael shrugged. "I think so, yes."

"Good. You need to get darker skin and hair first, then you and Juan need to get going."

"Okay, Mason." Michael stood up. Mason again felt like the walls shrank slightly. Michael always made rooms feel too small. He reached over and wiped Karen's tears away gently. She smiled up at him. "Let's go, babe. Ready, Mason?"

"Of course. The stuff is in the kitchen. Sorry you two don't get to kiss after that; our timeline is just too damn tight."

Juan smiled. "Yeah, Mikey, you could've had a lot more fun if you hadn't been so fucking stubborn!"

"Shut the fuck up, Johnny."

"Just saying, Mikey."

"You have a fucking big mouth. I am going to punch it closed for you."

"Nah, you won't. I am too fucking awesome for you to do something like that."

"Don't take any damn bets on that." Michael said ominously.

Mason sighed. "I almost wish you were still back there arguing. Then I wouldn't have to fucking listen to you two."

"Oh, you know you like it." Juan grinned impishly.

"No, not really. Not right now, at least."

"Oh, well, I can't help that." Juan shrugged and went over to the counter. "Who's hungry? Want something, Mikey?"

"Always."

"I thought so." Juan laughed and brought the food over to the table. "Here, you fucking idiot. I am going to run some blanks of different keys. We should be able to sneak in if there are locks."

"Michael, you are going to have to eat while I dye your hair." Mason said as he brought the supplies over. "Karen, you eat, too."

She nodded and took some flat bread. Michael smiled slightly at Mason. "Whatever, man, you just like bossing me around."

"No, not really, Michael, but it gets results from you. If you weren't so fucking set on being right at all costs, it wouldn't be such a fucking problem."

"I don't have to be right. I just am." Michael smiled, taking some more food.

Juan laughed loudly from where he was inspecting the blanks he'd printed. "Fuck no! You did not just play that card!"

"Oh, I did." Michael grinned at Juan and took some more flat bread.

Mason rolled his eyes at Karen and she laughed. "Have they always been this bad?" She asked.

"You have absolutely no fucking idea, Karen." Mason said in a long-suffering voice.

"Oh, poor Mason." She said mockingly.

"And now they are rubbing off on you. Damn."

"Nothing ever stays perfect." She said brightly. Juan and Michael laughed uproariously.

"You guys know I don't give a flying fuck about you making fun of me, but you're going to wake up Porter if you're too loud, so let's keep it down a little." Mason cautioned.

"Ooh, good call." Juan said seriously. "I forgot. Thank you for reminding me."

"You're welcome."

"I should probably go and check on Gabriella too. These blanks are pretty much done. Excuse me." He quietly left the room.

Mason turned back to Michael. "Well? Would you care to bitch about anything else now?" He asked as he pulled the dye components over and began mixing.

"Fuck you, Mason. You fucking know you've won."

"Actually, I don't know that, Michael. Are you going to do this right, or are you going to fight every damn decision I make?"

"No, I will do it. Karen made her choice, I will do it. You better make fucking good plans though."

"I intend to. Now, here is what you and Juan need to do. You need to get all the inside of that place mapped for me. I have a rough layout, but I need specifics. You've cased for me before; you know what I need to know. We have to get Karen and Gabriella inside, probably in some sort of wagon or caddy."

"Got it. Anything else?"

Mason started combing the dye through Michael's hair. "Well, I need as many details about it as you can get: where the men are, where the women are, where the guards are and their schedules. The usual stuff we need, but look specifically for a way to get the women in. I don't have a set plan for that yet and I need that tonight."

"Fine. Fuck!" Michael jerked his head to the side away from Mason. "You're pulling on purpose! Fucking hurts!" He accused loudly.

"Oh, shut the hell up, you big baby."

Karen was applying the skin dye to her arms and she laughed softly. "You two are amazing sometimes. If I didn't know better, I would think you were related, the way you fight. Either that or that you hate each other."

"Related? God, no!" Mason faked a shudder.

Michael snorted. "You are so damn dramatic sometimes."

"Whatever, man. I can get over my drama, big boy. I don't notice you making great inroads into your fucking problems yet."

"No? Well I am fucking trying!"

"No you're not! That's part of it. You think you are better but you aren't yet. Quit trying to get ahead of the therapist, idiot!"

Michael was silent for a few minutes. When he spoke again, it was quiet. "You are right, Mason, as usual. I hate being held back when I think I can do fucking better."

"I know, Michael." Mason said just as quietly. "Your therapist knows better than you do in this case. Let the experts tell you when you are ready."

Michael sighed heavily. "Damn it! Why can't it be easy?"

"I don't know. I'm sorry, Michael."

"I am sorry, too. I will try to do better."

"Good. This has to set. Let's dye your skin and you will be ready. You know what you and Juan need to do?"

"Yeah, as well as we can know, without being there."

"All right. Then let's get you done and gone."

Juan came out, Gabriella leaning on his arm. "Yeah, we do need to get. Where are the uniforms, Mason?" Mason gestured towards the counter vaguely and went back to dying Michael's face. "Uh, can you be more specific?" Juan asked.

"Juan, you know how to fucking open a damn bag and look!"

"Okay! Sheesh!" Juan helped Gabriella to the table and then began to dig through the bags. He pulled out several black burquas and tossed them aside. Then he pulled out some white uniforms and green head scarves. "Ha! Found them!"

Mason glanced over. "Yes, those green ones are for you. Those false beards are too. You know that the hardliners are all about the beards. The keffiyeh for Porter, James and me are red and white checked. You might not be able to get away after tonight. Once Karen and Gabriella are in, you both are not going to want to leave."

"Yeah, that's probably true. You're like smart and shit, Mason! Maybe you should be a doctor!"

"Maybe you should shut the hell up and get dressed, Johnny."

"Why didn't you give us these fucking beards first? It would be easier to not have to put everything on at once."

"So you could do your kissing and making up, idiot."

"Ooh, good point. I'll let it slide this time."

"Fuck you. And get done."

Juan had piled everything he and Michael would need on the table, shrugging, and started unbuttoning his shirt and jeans. Gabriella raised her eyebrow at him. "Aren't you going to go somewhere else to do that?"

49

"Why? We have to get going as soon as possible and once Mikey is all done, we are outta here."

"Hey, it's not like I fucking mind seeing your body."

"Good!" Juan pulled his shirt off.

"Hot damn."

Karen whistled. "Hot damn is right. Are all engineers that built?"

"Of course not." Juan grinned as he pulled on the tunic. "No more than most contractors are built like Mikey or jewelers like Porter. We just fucking blessed!"

Karen shook her head. "No, we're the blessed ones."

Juan laughed. "You are one lucky guy, Mikey." He said to Michael as he adjusted his tunic.

"No shit, Johnny. Am I done, Mason?"

"Let's wash the hair out and you should be fine." Mason assured him.

Chapter 7

Once Michael and Juan had left, Mason turned to Karen. "You're next. Come over here and I will do it."

"Just promise not to pull my hair." She teased.

"Yeah, you know, I am not into that sort of thing. You and Michael can do what you want but keep it private, please."

Karen blushed very red. Gabriella laughed. "Nice, Mason."

Mason shrugged. "I find that making jokes is a good way to avoid getting stressed. Ready, Karen?"

"Do I have any choice?"

"Of course you do. You always have a choice."

"Oh. Well, then, yes, I am ready."

It didn't take very long to get Karen's hair dyed. Mason sat at the table with both Gabriella and her as her hair set. "Here's how this is probably going to have to work, ladies. Michael and Juan will come back at the end of their shift. They have both done this type of thing before, so they know what to look for and what type of things I need to know. We can't move before they get back. We'll know best how to get you ladies in. Once you're in, they aren't going to be able to get information to me at all. They will want to stay and make sure you're good."

"Got it, Mason." Gabriella said. "How are we supposed to act?"

"Women are supposed to wear a burqua at all times in the presence of strange men, except when Emil decides to auction. Then he has them put on alluring clothes under the burqua and takes the burqua off on the sale stand."

"Like a strip show?" Gabriella sounded disgusted.

"Sort of. Anyway, that is beside the point, because you won't get there. In fact, I am going to cause a hell of a disturbance so that Sienna and Callie don't get sold. It may involve fatalities, especially Emil the Madman. I plan to have the UN move on the Army of the Almighty before any deals can be finalized but after the sale starts. It is a human rights violation, so they are willing to back us. They'll come in when we signal. I want you two to get the women to your side. They must be willing to

51

swarm the guards and get the men out. A lot of these women are being sold from their lawful marriages, and they are going to be pissed about that. If we can get them to riot enough, not too much, we can turn the Army of the Almighty into a punch-line. They want to be taken seriously, but if you two can convince the women in there that they can act, what is to stop anyone else from acting against them?"

Karen nodded. "If they are trying to intimidate people, it won't work if they are not successful here."

"Exactly. So, that is what you two are up against. We're going to wash your hair, Karen, then we are going to practice some accents. If Porter wakes up, he can help. Ready?"

They both nodded. Mason smiled slightly. "I know it seems a bit scary, but you are both perfect for this. I would never ask it of anyone I thought couldn't handle it, and do it perfectly."

Karen smiled weakly. "Thanks, Mason."

They practiced for about an hour speaking with the accents Mason thought they could adopt easily. It was going quite well. Porter wandered in after he had slept for about two hours. He was looking for water.

"How do they sound to you?" Mason asked quietly as they stood back listening to Gabriella and Karen conversing.

Porter drank his water slowly, listening closely. "Pretty good, Mason. Very good, actually. Karen should be a little harsher though. She is too soft."

"I meant her voice, Porter."

Porter laughed. "So did I, Mason, but you know that."

"Of course I did. I only wanted to make you laugh. How are you doing?"

"Okay." Porter said soberly. "I had some bad nightmares though. And I have the feeling that they took her rings away."

"They probably did. They could get tons of money for those."

"I know. Oh well. They're just rocks anyway."

They stood listening a little longer. "You should probably get some more sleep, Porter." Mason cautioned.

"I know, I know." Porter sighed wearily.

"I will be in there soon, maybe in another hour."

"Great. Can't wait to hear your fucking snores."

"I don't fucking snore." Mason protested. Porter snorted derisively. "I don't. Michael does."

"Yeah, whatever, fairy princess. See you later."

Mason smiled slightly. "I will be there, Porter. Count on it. And on me."

Porter nodded, still watching Gabriella and Karen. His eyes were much brighter than usual. He glanced at Mason quickly and left.

Mason shook his head. This Emil was in some serious shit for this. Mason didn't take kindly to people fucking his friends over. He had to stop that idiot as soon as possible or he would escalate. It had happened more times that way than Mason could conveniently count. If the world took notice and became outraged over something perpetrated by a warlord, the next one tried to be more outrageous and disgusting. Media types were always looking for the next big headline to scream at people. Mason didn't like that. He tried to stay away from journalists as much as possible. There was usually some agenda they were working towards and Mason would be no one's pawn.

"All right, ladies. Pack it in. We're done for now. Karen, try to be a little harsher in accent, but otherwise, you two are ready. Get some sleep."

They both nodded and left. Mason got himself some water and sat, drinking in the silence and stillness. He relished the quiet. It helped center him. The next few days were going to be very taxing. Porter was going to be pushing himself far too hard, and James would probably do the same. Neither of them was good at being moderate when it involved the women. Actually, Mason was a little surprised that Porter was being semi-logical about this. He had expected to be fighting to keep the man in bed and not out hunting Emil single-handedly.

He could probably assassinate the Army leader on his own, too. It was extracting him that would be the problem. Porter was good, very good, but he was one man, and Mason doubted that they would be able to get him out if he went it alone. It would be too public and too easy to trace. By storming the slave auction, there would be enough cover to keep it anonymous.

He sighed and stood up. Bed was definitely overdue. Mason left the lights on in the kitchen area. He didn't know when Michael and Juan might show up.

He slipped back into the room Porter and James were sleeping in. James was clearly exhausted. He was sleeping so hard that Mason was pretty sure he hadn't even turned over. Porter was sleeping lightly. He almost never slept hard.

Mason quietly got into some blankets in an unoccupied corner. Although he wasn't an orthodox believer himself, he knew that Porter valued his Catholic roots, and he thought something like a prayer towards Porter's God might help. The soft breathing in the room eventually lulled him to sleep.

It was later when Porter woke up. It had been a terrible nightmare, that much was obvious, and Mason had a hell of time calming him back down. After five minutes of soothing talk, Porter relaxed.

"Fucking hell." He murmured, letting go of Mason's arms finally and laying back.

"That was kind of intense." Mason observed, pulling the blankets back up and over Porter.

"Must have been."

"You don't remember?" Mason asked a bit incredulously. His arms still hurt from where Porter had squeezed the hell out of them.

"No, but that is probably a good thing."

"It might be. You gonna be okay?"

Porter took a long, shuddering breath. "I think so. Thanks for being here."

"No problem. You are fucking crazy enough for me to justify it."

Porter smiled slightly. "No kidding."

"You need more sleep. We don't have four hours, so you have to do it on your own."

"Okay, Mason. I will try."

"Good. I will be here if you need."

Porter relaxed further. "I know."

Mason went back to his own bed and listened for a few minutes. Porter seemed to be close to sleep again, which was good. Of course, he could be faking it and Mason wouldn't be able to tell; just rest would help, too. Porter was very important to Mason as a friend as well as a team member. He had to get better quickly. Mason needed him even as Porter needed Mason.

Mason drifted back to sleep. When he woke up again, it was morning. Porter's bed was empty, which was no surprise; he was usually the first person up. James was still asleep, although he seemed close to being awake. Mason got up quietly.

Porter was in the kitchen, getting food ready. He liked cooking, and it gave him something constructive to do.

"Morning, sunshine." Mason yawned. He accepted a cup of very strong coffee and sat at the table.

"Good morning, princess." Porter returned softly. "Was I that bad last night?"

"No, probably not. I was up too late with the ladies though. That one time was all you had."

"I don't really remember."

"That's probably just as well."

Porter nodded and kept making food. "Well, thanks, Mason. I appreclate you keeping me in line."

Mason snorted softly. "Fuck that. I love you too much, fucking ass."

Porter laughed. "Lucky for me!"

"Yes, lucky for you. What are you making, anyway?"

"Eggs. Yogurt. Shit like that."

"Good. I can't wait." Mason yawned again and drank some more coffee.

"You don't have to." Porter brought two plates over and sat down.

"Awesome." Mason poked at the food curiously. "It smells pretty good, Porter. I'm impressed."

Porter shrugged. "Whatever. When are Michael and Juan getting in?"

"I have no idea. I don't have a schedule for this situation. Amazingly, the Moroccan government didn't have many details of the Army of the Almighty."

"That fucking stands to reason, Mason."

"I don't want to be fucking reasonable, Porter. I want answers."

"Oh, poor boy." Porter said mockingly. "You will just have to be patient."

"Like you are some fucking expert on that."

"Yeah, you're right. Let's eat and argue about it later."

Mason shrugged and started eating. The argument meant next to nothing to him. He was much more interested in Porter being able to respond.

James shambled out soon, looking decidedly unhappy. Porter gave him some food with no comment.

"Coffee, please." James said softly.

"Since when do you drink coffee?" Porter asked, pouring a cup.

"Since I can't fall asleep today and dream about her again."

Mason sighed. "Okay, don't you two start. Not until we get the recon. James, we need to darken your hair and skin. There is no way to get you in looking like you do now. I will do your hair while you eat."

James nodded wearily. Mason was fairly sure that his exhaustion had little to do with physical exertion. He mixed the dyes quickly and colored James' hair black.

James ate without appearing to notice what he was doing. Mason was going to have to address that, probably once the caffeine kicked in. Porter also seemed to notice. He glanced at Mason knowingly.

56

"I'm going to go wash up. See you in a few minutes." He said artlessly. James didn't respond.

Once Porter was gone, Mason removed James' plate from in front of him. "All right, we are going to face up to this now. You must talk to me, James."

"What about?"

"You are unresponsive. I can't have you acting this wooden in a dangerous situation; you could expose us all. We'd all be dead. If you can't be human, you can't come. Right now you are as mechanical and stiff as a robot."

"I can't help it, Mason. I feel like I am stuck in a pool of jelly or something. I keep trying to care and interact, but I can't quite do it. It is like I am outside myself, watching some puppeteer move me around. It is frankly weird."

Mason nodded slowly. "That is probably your mind trying to insulate you from your emotional responses. Unfortunately, it is doing too good a job. I need you to be able to react, and right now you are incapable of that."

"What can I do, Dr. Briggs? I need to help."

"I know you do. Perhaps we can do some guided exercises to help you reconnect."

James nodded. "That sounds good to me."

"We'll need Porter. He was there."

"Is it like hypnotism or something?"

"Sort of. Let me get Porter and we will do one or two things. You need to relax as totally as you can. Deep, measured breaths. Close your eyes. Just think and float. I'll be right back."

Porter was sitting in the room staring at the wall. He looked up when Mason touched his shoulder. "How's it going?"

Mason shook his head. "Not well. We are going to do some guided exercises. You have to be there because you know the details."

"Ah, fuck, you know I hate those."

"Too bad. He needs to relive and re-feel it all. He is so far insulated right now that I don't know if he is even consciously aware of what has happened. Besides, it will help you, too. Get your ass up."

"Yeah, yeah, get off me, bitch. I am getting." He stood up slowly. Then he shook his head. "That damn side is gonna be a fucking problem, Mason. I keep forgetting about it."

"Can't really help that, Porter. Besides, I don't want you so fixated on it that you ignore other stuff."

"Yeah, okay, good point."

"Go warn the ladies to not interrupt us. That could be a big problem."

"What, you want me to tell them to stay in their rooms?"

Mason shrugged. "I don't give a flying fuck, I just don't want them talking in the middle of this. They can choose whether to watch or not."

"All right, sheesh, you are fucking touchy as hell this morning."

"Fuck off."

"Just noting it is all. Be right there."

Chapter 8

Mason went back to the kitchen after he had retrieved his small medical pouch. This promised to be moderately uncomfortable for him, and more than a little hard for Porter. It was the only way he could do it here quickly enough to make a difference. He set the pouch on the table beside James.

"Roll up your sleeve." He instructed as he loaded a syringe.

"Why? What's that?" James asked even as he unbuttoned and rolled his sleeve up.

"It's something to help with this. The scientific name won't mean jack shit to you."

"Is it some truth drug?"

"No, there isn't such thing as a truth drug. It will help you be less inhibited, and that might make this easier. If nothing else, it will help you to reconnect yourself with yourself." Mason carefully inserted the hypodermic into James' arm and slowly injected him. "Now we have to wait a few minutes. We have to wait for Porter anyway. He needs to be here, since he was there."

"Okay, whatever." James was still very indifferent. "I don't think anything will help. You'll just have to leave me."

"Fuck that!" Mason was getting irritated, which was probably a bad thing. It was just too much for him now. "Fuck it all! I don't fucking leave anybody the fuck behind! If you can't fucking pull it together, you can fucking go to hell! I am not in any fucking position to deal with this shit from you."

"Damn." Porter said drily from right behind him. "I haven't heard you lose it this badly in a long time."

"Shut the fuck up and sit the fuck down now."

"Sir!" Porter did sit, very quickly.

Mason knew he was being a little ridiculous about all this, but he was exasperated by everything that was out of his control. "Porter, honestly..."

Porter winked at him. "I know, I know. I am sorry. It merely surprised me."

Mason smiled in spite of his bad mood. "Apology accepted, you ass." He looked closely at James. It looked like the stuff was taking effect. "Let's do this, then. I need you to close your eyes. Breathe in, deeply. Imagine it going all through your body, down to your toes. Breathe it all out. Empty your lungs, then keep going. Breathe in and imagine it cleansing your body. Breathe out all toxins. Breathe in. Breathe out. Relax. You are going to be all right. You must focus on the breathing only. Feel it, exist in it, become it." Mason was quiet for a few seconds, watching as James visibly relaxed. His face looked less wooden, more human. Good. Time to get this fucking mess taken care of. "All right. I need you to start going back in your memory. Go back to Mahmoud's office. What did it look like? Find where the desk was. You see it there? The wood grain is very fine, the varnish is old but beautiful. The chair you were in, do you see it? Which was it?"

James slowly inhaled. "The far right one. It had bronze work that intrigued me. Callie had the one right to my left. It was a little smaller, and she seemed to like it."

"Good, James. Very good. What did Mahmoud do after you had looked over the diamonds?"

James' forehead wrinkled as he concentrated. "Uh, I don't really remember."

Mason glanced at Porter. "We were going to discuss the prices. James, you wanted to add a bonus. You were ready to close." Porter said softly. His hands were tightly clenched on the table. Mason knew he was having trouble with this. It was going to get worse. Porter had been through this type of exercise before, and he knew what was coming. Mason felt sorry for him but they had to get James better.

James smiled a tiny smile. "Oh, that is right. You were a bit skeptical about two of the stones, sir. You thought they had inclusions that would be insurmountable. I don't think so. They have such character. I want those two." He had shifted to present tense. Good. This was going well enough. James was reliving it as if it was happening

60

again. Gabriella and Karen had come in at some point very quietly. Mason hadn't even noticed them.

"Very good, James. They are beautiful stones, aren't they?"

James nodded eagerly. "The inclusions could work for them, if they are handled correctly. Porter is a perfectionist, and he may not see the possibilities they hold. He won't argue with me about it though. He is willing to trust my judgment. I am grateful for that. I hope I won't let him down."

"No, James, you won't." Porter whispered, tears in his eyes again.

James didn't seem to hear. "Mahmoud is very excited. He doesn't try to hide his feelings from us at all. I know he wants us to be repeat buyers. If he can provide this type of stone again, there should be no problem with that."

Mason glanced at his watch. Juan and Michael came into the kitchen. Juan put his hand on Michael's chest in warning and they stayed silent. Mason was suddenly filled with gratitude. He had to keep going, and they realized it and respected him. "Mahmoud is very excited to have you there. What happens next?"

James looks a little confused. "Uh, well, he seems a little sad to let the stones go. I think he really enjoys what he does. I get the sense that he cares less about the money than the diamonds themselves. He seems like a very genuine person. I could be wrong about that. Sometimes, I take people at face value and I am wrong. It is problem I have. Mahmoud could take us for a ride, it is true. I hope he doesn't. I think he is very glad to have us interested. He drags some of the negotiations out just to get to know us better, I think."

Porter drew a ragged breath. "Then there is a knock at the door. Mahmoud looks very surprised, a little angry even. He looks towards the door and back at us, saying he left orders to not be interrupted." Tears had run down his face. His eyes were closed tightly.

James nodded. "Mahmoud apologizes and stands up. He is upset. He goes to the door. He says something about leaving orders, and he opens the door to chastise whomever it is the hall. But he never

61

does."

"No, he doesn't." Porter says softly. "There are two, possibly three rifle shots. There must be at least three separate people in the hall outside."

"Mahmoud falls back into the room. He has a bullet hole in his head. Blood is coming from it." James began to look upset. He also began to move restlessly in his seat, as if reliving it has caused him to want to fight back now. "The men in the hall push their way into the room. When the rifles went off, Porter had already thrown himself out of his chair and forced Sienna and Callie down. I am too late. I see the men look at the diamonds on the desk first. Then they see us. They look surprised, then greedy. I think they wanted the diamonds at first, but now they want something else. But I am too late to stop them from taking the diamonds. I am too late to stop them from shooting Mahmoud. I can't even protect Callie from any more shots."

"Stop for a moment, James." Mason said soothingly. "You have already lived all this. You cannot change any of it. Nothing you have done is your fault now. You have to accept what happened. You have to accept what you may or may not have done. Most of all, you must understand why you were there. Why were you there, James? You had a reason. What reason? You had something you could do and only you could do it. What was it? You must find it, James. We need you to remember what it was that you saw and experienced."

James thought for a moment or two. "Maybe I was there to see what they came for. Porter doesn't see; he is taking care of the women. I see the men look for the diamonds first. Porter doesn't see that. The men scoop all the loose diamonds into a bag on the desk. They make sure they get everything without any regard for what they are grabbing. Those diamonds are valuable, but they are not equal. Many are much lesser stones. The men don't seem to care. They must want diamonds, any diamonds and they don't want just the best. Porter would never grab like that. But he doesn't see it. He keeps them safe. I wish I could keep her safe."

"You did what you needed to do, James. What do the men do after they see you?"

"They call out the door. They say something about someone wanting to see this. Another man comes in. He doesn't have a head scarf or anything over his face. He smiles at us. He wants the women. I see him look at them like he looks at the diamond bag. He is greedy. He takes the bag of diamonds that the other men have taken from Mahmoud's desk. He doesn't even look in it though. He is still looking at the women. He still wants more. He tells the men to kill Porter and myself. They shoot me, I feel it. I fall back, but my head hits something. There are more shots. I can't tell how many. Maybe they have shot Porter. Maybe he is dead. I am not dying, but it hurts. My head hurts where it hit whatever it hit. The room is going black, but I know I hear Callie and Sienna screaming. I need to stay awake! They need me; she needs me. I fight the black, but it takes over. I tried; Callie, I am so sorry!" James started crying with shocking suddenness.

Mason was not alarmed; he knew that James had allowed himself to realize both what he could and could not do. It was important that he learn to accept that he was not some sort of superhero and that he was fine the way he was. James measured himself unconsciously to Porter all the time. He had to realize that he was not Porter, which was just as well: Mason didn't think he could handle another Porter. James was strong in other ways. He had to learn it. Acceptance was a bitch but it had to happen before anyone could move on. Of course, that included Porter, who was probably pissed about this all again.

Under his altered skin-tone, Porter had gone deathly pale again. "God damn it, Mason, can we be fucking done now? I made shitloads of mistakes, and she is gone because of them. I'd rather not be incapacitated by regret."

"Yes, we can be done, but shit, Porter, what the hell would you have done differently, anyway? No one can ever say how things might have been. You know all this. You are smart enough."

Porter nodded. "Fuck, I know. And yet..."

"I understand, but dammit Porter, you really need to get over that. James, please focus again on your breathing. You breathe in cleansing, healing air. You breathe out and the regret leaves you. You are whole, you are worthy. You breathe in, taking in all the living air from trees miles away. You breathe out, connected with the entire world. You are vital to the world. You matter, just because you exist, and because you are you. Breathe in, James." Mason watched as he calmed and finally stopped sobbing. "We are not here to judge. None of us can do that. You have done what you needed to do, and things were things that only you could do. You need to realize just how special you are as yourself. Now, James, we need you. Will you help us?"

James opened his eyes slowly. He seemed to have trouble focusing them for a moment. Then he smiled a tiny smile at Mason. "Of course, Dr. Briggs. I can't let you down, too."

Mason shook his head. "No, James, you have let no one down. And you won't start now. Do you understand what I am telling you? You don't have to believe me, not yet, but you have to hear it." He waited until James nodded. "All right, now that shit's over, who's hungry?"

"Nice segue." Michael grunted. "That must have been one hell of shithole to be in, Porter. I'm really sorry, man." He reached out and roughly grasped porter's shoulder.

"You have no fucking idea, man." Porter said, breathing deeply himself. "Worst shit ever. I was pretty sure I would be doing my fucking time in Purgatory a lot sooner than I had anticipated, and I think I will be spending damn near eternity there anyway."

Juan shook his head. "Fucking not how anyone should spend the day they get married."

"No, I can definitely recommend you skip it." Porter sniffed loudly and wiped his eyes.

James also wiped his eyes. "I am really sorry, sir."

"James, would you use my goddamn fucking name? And did you not fucking hear Mason? You saw things I couldn't. Because you were paying attention, he knows how to fucking proceed. Now shut the fuck up. There is nothing, absolutely nothing, to be sorry for."

James sighed. He clearly didn't believe it. Juan grinned at him. "Porter, don't fucking sugar-coat it, man; tell him exactly what you fucking think!"

Porter smiled wanly back. "Johnny boy, you are a treasure." He stood up and went to the sink.

"Well, that wasn't quite the response I expected." Juan observed.

"It's the fucking truth anyway." Michael said calmly.

"That's way closer to what I thought Porter would say. Thanks for stepping up, Mikey. The level of swearing was just far too low."

Michael sighed theatrically and shook his head in mock annoyance.

"Oh, is that all you wanted?" Porter said over his shoulder. "I can always add lots of spare words in. I didn't realize there was demand for that."

"Porter, there is always demand for that."

Karen sighed. "Is there any way to tame them?" She asked Gabriella despairingly.

Gabriella smiled. "I doubt it, but you knew that."

"A girl can always hope."

Chapter 9

Porter quickly produced more of what he and Mason had already had. James got another plate, since he hadn't eaten more than half his first one. He seemed more receptive and more awake. Both were encouraging to Mason.

"Talk to me, Johnny; I need information." Mason said as Juan started shoveling food. "Do it while you hog your food down, please. We don't have lots of time before you need to get back."

Juan nodded and swallowed an enormous mouthful. He took a long drink of coffee. "God, Porter, this is some good shit!" He congratulated Porter.

Porter nodded solemnly. "Thank you, kind sir."

Juan pulled the notebook Mason had out over. He sketched a quick map out with one hand while he ate flatbread in with the other. "Okay, so here's the general layout. Pens are over here, soldier barracks here and there, kitchen here, showers and bathrooms here. Emil's house is here, in front. Michael and I were able to get in, no sweat. The guy on duty actually was asleep. So that was fine. The cart they use to wheel the slop around was pretty rickety." Juan paused to shove more food in.

"Was?" Mason prompted impatiently. He didn't have time to watch Juan scarf his food down.

Michael grinned evilly. "Yeah, would you believe that the handles both fell off, together, at the same time? Fucking amazing coincidence. I only had to push on them four times to get them to break."

"Coincidence. Uh-huh." Mason said drily. "I assume you brought it here to fix it?"

"Why, Mason, you didn't expect us to fucking leave them a broken cart, now did you? That wouldn't be very neighborly." Michael smirked. "Actually, Juan had to act pretty sorry. He kept apologizing over and over about it and promised to get it fixed right away. It was fucking hilarious to watch him fawning and scraping and shit."

Juan shook his head sourly. "Shut up, Mikey. Like anyone would buy you trying to act sorry for anything."

"Later, boys." Mason snapped. "Can it be modified to get the ladies in?"

Michael nodded. "It'll do fine, Mason. It'll need a little welding to strengthen the frame and the handles, but it has lots of useless space. Fucking poor engineering."

Juan shrugged. "Not everyone is an expert at efficiency. Actually, Mason, we couldn't have designed one better for this." Michael snorted. "Okay, maybe we could, but I don't think so." Juan amended airily. "The point is that it will work quite well, provided it can handle the weight. Michael and I will start on that right after food."

"I'll help." Porter offered.

"Thanks." Juan said simply. "You are the best at spotting potential problems."

"That I doubt, but I am what you have to work with. You spot much more than I ever do, Johnny."

Juan shrugged again. He clearly was more interested in eating than arguing. He depleted his food in an alarmingly short time.

"You know that if you had fucking eaten last night you wouldn't be so hungry today, right?" Mason asked pointedly.

Juan smiled. "Mason, save the lecture for someone who both fucking cares and who can fucking change. When I is stressed, I don't eats. Shut the hell up about it."

"You need serious help."

"I do not think there is a damn thing anyone can do about it, except keep me from getting stressed, and we all know that won't happen. Just let me deal with it my way, Mason. You can fucking yell at me if it goes too far."

"Why, so you can fucking ignore me more?"

"Yeah, pretty much." Juan stood up. "Well, boys, it's been fun, but we have a cart to fix. It has to be ready in an hour. Let's get going."

Michael grabbed a little more flatbread and shoved it into his pocket. "Just a second, Johnny." He also shoveled the rest of his eggs in. Chewing mightily, he and Juan left the kitchen.

Porter shook his head in despair. "I should learn to care less. They never linger over the food. Makes me feel useless sometimes."

Karen smiled and laid her hand on Porter's arm. "It doesn't mean they don't appreciate it, Porter."

He smiled sadly at her. "No, I suppose not. Well, charming lady, I did say I would help. Perhaps it will erase some of the pain of the little exercise that Mason ran."

"But it wasn't that hard, Porter."

"Ah, my lovely Karen that depends exclusively on where you were sitting I assure you." Porter bowed to them all and also left the kitchen.

"How would a different seat make any difference?" Karen asked blankly.

Gabriella smiled gently. "He meant who the person is, not where they were sitting."

Karen flushed slowly. "Oh. I am not very good with figurative language still." She said ruefully.

"Karen, it is okay. Porter sometimes hides his emotions behind language."

Mason nodded vigorously. "He does indeed! One of his many problems. Although I think I prefer that to his hiding it in silence, right, James?"

James sighed. "Yes, I know what you are referring to, Dr. Briggs."

"How do you feel?"

"Like hell. I still feel like I let her down."

"James, you're still alive. Unless you are fucking dead, there is always something you can do to rectify the situation."

"I guess I hadn't considered that."

"Do. Please. I need your help almost exclusively at this point."

"Mine?" James was very surprised. "Why me? Why not Porter?"

"Two reasons, James. One is that you are here, and more importantly, you saw these bastards. You watched them much more closely and impartially than Porter did. He was observing from the floor, with his mind already shut most of the way off. He always does that in stressful situations. It helps in some ways, but it is a huge impediment in others."

"Ah, I see." James sighed again. "Very well, Dr. Briggs. What do you want?"

"First, James, use my goddamn name." Gabriella snickered. Mason shot her a nasty look. "There is an actual reason for that, but right now, it just wastes time."

"Fine, Mason."

"Good. Now, tell me how they acted and spoke. As clearly as you can. Close your eyes and focus on the guys, not what they were doing or what happened next."

Obediently, James closed his eyes. "Well, let's see. The first ones through the door were wearing head scarves and face coverings, and some had sunglasses. I couldn't see anything at all."

"What color?"

"The scarves were green, like the ones Juan and Michael had on earlier."

"Excellent. Then?"

"They had rifles, but I don't know what type. Not hunting rifles."

"All right. I assume they held them professionally?"

"Um…" James thought for a moment. "One of them held it in his right hand, the other one held it kind of off to his left side and he seemed less competent, more like he was acting a part or something. He seemed to hold it almost like it was a baseball bat or something."

"Very good. Voices?"

"They all spoke English. I know you said that is because they only have that as a common language. There were a total of five guys who came in, including Emil. But some of them spoke English better than others. One of them I could hardly understand at all, and Emil spoke excellently. Very fluent and used slang language easily."

Mason nodded. "Very good, James. Anything else?"

James thought again, his forehead furrowing. "I don't know how this might help, but it seemed like his men didn't hold Emil in high regard.

I got the impression that they didn't think he was great leader only because he gave them something they wanted, or maybe because they are afraid to disobey. It is just my guess, Mason. I can't base it on anything."

"James, I trust your instincts. I asked you for that. I need your impressions, and what you got from those impressions. Thank you. You can try and make peace with this all now. I suggest you go and lie down for a little while. You don't have to sleep, but just do whatever you need to do to get better. Prayer, meditation, whatever."

James sighed heavily. "All right, Mason."

"Oh, and James?" Mason said, already distracted by an idea that was forming. James turned in the doorway. "Crying is normal and healthy, so don't be afraid of it, especially if you are alone. See you in a while." James left but Mason was already thinking ahead to something else, something with real possibilities.

If Emil's men weren't all fanatically attached, that could work. They would not be willing to die for their leader. They were in it for gain of some sort, whatever it was. It could be money, women, diamonds, faith, any of them, but if they could be soured on Emil, that might be just as useful in the end for Mason as military intervention. He'd have to think on this angle a bit more.

Still thinking distractedly, Mason gestured to Karen and Gabriella. "Start talking, ladies, and use your accents. You will start to identify those accents with your characters. Get dressed in the burquas. That will also help you two identify. And hurry up; you only have fifteen fucking minutes to be done."

"Of course, Mason!" Gabriella said hurriedly. They both stood up and began to put on the black clothes, speaking softly in their accented voices.

Mason pulled his small notebook back over. He started to jot down ideas. Porter was probably going to kill Emil. If he didn't, someone else was going to. That was kind of a given. The man was too fucking unstable to let him wander around without anyone checking him. The UN would take care of it if Porter didn't or couldn't. So Emil would be gone. Mason wanted to avoid making him into a martyr to any sort of ideal. The women that Gabriella and Karen were going to stir up would help there. The men were in charge, but the women were able to subversively influence things. There must be some way to keep the power from going to another single fanatical leader again.

Mason seemed to remember that there were three generals in the Army of the Almighty. None of them were bad choices for this, but Mason wanted even more instability. He wanted the lieutenants to be grabbing for their own piece of the action. He wanted Juan and Michael to stir up intrigue there. If the soldiers were distrustful of each leader, they would be much harder to unite behind one. That was what Mason wanted. He couldn't get rid of every warlord, but he could weaken them by dividing their troops in loyalties. Mason was uninterested who they backed. He merely wanted them dispersed. He wasn't trying to advance an agenda. Morocco would have to fucking fix itself; he just wanted to give it more of a chance to be able to do it.

"Mason?" One of the ladies asked him tentatively. He couldn't really tell which.

"Yes? Sorry, I was thinking about something."

"Obviously." It had to be Gabriella. "I asked how we look."

"Exceptionally anonymous. In other words, perfect."

"Oh good. I would hate to be this hot for no reason. I'm already sweating."

"Yes, and it will only get worse, I am afraid. The good news is that it is only for a day more."

"Hooray."

Porter, Juan and Michael came in. They looked the ladies over quickly. Juan nodded. "Perfect, Mason. Just make sure you don't make any eye contact with men, ladies. That's a complete no-no. It could get you shot." Juan was not serious too often and when he was it added emphasis. Everyone took him at his word.

"Juan and Michael, I have more for you to do." Mason said.

"What? Fuck, Mason. You haven't given us enough yet?"

"Shut the fuck up. I need you two to spread dissent in the ranks of the soldiery. I don't want them all backing one leader again."

"Wait," Michael said quickly, "They are allied behind Emil right now."

"I have it on good authority that Emil is going to break out in a rash of mortality tomorrow."

"You gave Porter his knives, didn't you?" It wasn't really a question. Porter smiled slightly at the implication.

Mason shrugged. "It seemed like a good idea at the time."

"Sure, but which time?"

"It really doesn't much matter. Someone is going to kill that man; it might be Porter, it might be the UN, it might be one of his generals. I don't much care. Spread ill-will, boys. Go on. And when the sale goes down, Michael, you have to signal the UN. Lift your rifle three times and then you and Juan have to take out all the guards. They can't be tied up getting in. It will warn too many inside if they are."

"Sir!" Juan drew himself up stiffly and threw a salute. "Let's go, Mikey. We have to get the ladies in that thing and back before midday prayers."

The small group exited. Porter sat down opposite Mason with a sigh. "I'm glad to be doing something."

"We will be on shortly, I assure you. Then you'll be acting to your little heart's content."

Porter nodded. "How's James doing?"

"He's all right, I think. That sort of thing is very hard on people, as you well know."

"God, yes. I hate that stuff. It makes me question every movement I have made."

"That isn't what it is supposed to do, you ass."

"I know, Mason, but it does anyway. It makes me feel like I should be looking for where I made mistakes."

"You idiot. You have to be so victim-stance on everything, even to the point that you make yourself a victim on purpose."

"Yeah, thanks, Mason. That is gonna cure me for sure." Porter said with heavy sarcasm.

"Well, you need to stop. Sometimes being blunt helps you."

"I suppose that is true. Should we go and check on James?"

"Probably. We need to present ourselves for our initial interview as buyers."

Chapter 10

James was doing better, Mason could see that immediately. Even though he had obviously cried, he was responsive and alert, both of which Mason needed. James had good instincts; Mason would be relying on him and Porter for this to come off. He looked around quickly and stood up when he saw Porter and Mason standing in the doorway.

"Ready, Doctor?" He asked.

Mason sighed heavily. "James, really?"

"I only did it to make you roll your eyes. I am a little hungry. Is there any food left?"

Porter smiled. "Well, Juan and Michael have already left. There might be some crumbs lying around somewhere in the kitchen."

"Let's go and look, sir."

"James…" Porter said warningly.

"Yes, I know, Porter. I forgot."

Yes, Mason decided, he was definitely better than he had been. "Come on and we'll get you two fed. Then we have to go and present our credentials for the slave markets."

"Do we have credentials? That was fucking quick." Porter asked curiously. It usually took hours to get paperwork forged.

"We do, but we really only have to have one important one."

"Which is?"

Mason smiled. "Gold and diamonds, Porter; what did you think? Gold and diamonds will buy anything here."

"I hope these aren't quality stones."

Mason shrugged. "We aren't really buying anything, so it won't matter. I don't know how good the stones are, although I've been assured that they aren't high quality. I just know we have a shit-load of them, they are rough, and we have gold."

"Okay, I got it. Here, James, here's some bread with apricot stuff. You'll need both sugar and salt after that sort of experience."

James nodded. Then he did something rather surprising. He reached over and hugged Porter. "We'll get them back, Porter."

Porter looked alarmed, but he accepted the embrace with enough grace. "I know it, James. I am thinking we will just have to destroy this goddamn Army of the Almighty, too. I have it on some of the best authority that God does not speak through crazy-ass egotistical maniacs."

James smiled up at Porter. "Who said that?"

"The Vatican." Porter grinned. "I figure that is good enough for me."

"I don't think the Church has said anything about the Army of the Almighty, Porter." Mason protested.

"I never mentioned the Army specifically, Mason, I said egotistical maniacs. She has spoken many times against those."

"Okay okay, I concede your point. Now, here are our clothes. We'd best get changed. Oh, and gentlemen, there is a remote possibility that we will have to see the merchandise today. Do not, under any circumstance, let it show that you know those girls in there. They'll make sure none of us leave alive if you do."

Porter sighed. "Oh, fuck. I hope not."

"Then you had better start praying hard to whoever it is who is in charge of this sort of thing. I can't tell you who to go to for a fucked up thing like this. I am not really up on my patron saints, sorry."

"The only one I know of who might apply is the Jesuit Peter Claver."

"Good enough. I always did like the Jesuits. Hell, ask any saint you are on good terms with to help out."

"You can ask, too, Mason. God doesn't mind listening to fucking heathens occasionally."

Mason laughed. He finished adjusting his robes and put on his keffiyeh. Porter also put his disguise on, although the long flowing pants were a bit short. James smiled at that. "Ever considered shrinking, Porter?"

"Fucking shut up. Of course I have. It is fucking hard being this tall. Everyone notices tall men."

Mason rolled his eyes in resignation. "Whatever. You have lived with it how long now? Just fucking get going. We can bicker later."

James laughed as he put on his own tunic and keffiyeh. Mason was very relieved to hear that. Laughter was important, maybe even more important than crying.

"All right, you two fucking morons ready?" Mason demanded. "I don't have all day to listen to you two make bad jokes."

Porter struck a theatrical pose. "Mason! I am shocked! We don't make bad jokes!"

James laughed again. Mason shook his head. "You know what, Porter? Just start walking. I am not even going to dignify that with a response."

"What? We don't."

"Fucking walk, Porter!"

"I don't see why you are all pissed at me, Mason. It was your mistake."

Mason put his hand flat on Porter's chest warningly. "Either start walking or I pull your own damn knife on you and make you. Now move, bitch!"

Porter laughed and turned towards the door. "He is pissy as all hell, ain't he?" He winked towards James.

"It must be the yoghurt. I bet it doesn't agree with his delicate constitution." James said with a straight face.

"Excellent observation, James. Is that it, Mason? It your little tummy upset from yoghurt?"

"Nope, it is the shit I have to endure from idiots like you two, now walk!" Mason said shortly.

"Chill, Mason, we are walking, we are walking!" Porter said soothingly.

Mason was, in truth, not at all worried about the time. They needed to get there but there was no set time to show. He did want to make sure Porter and James didn't have time to regress. He couldn't afford to lose them now, especially not since they were both doing so much better in the face of unbelievable loss.

76

They made their way quietly through the narrow streets. Mason had to check their progress with his map once or twice. They got to Emil's fortress a little before noon. There were several other groups of men going into the main entrance.

Porter looked the other groups over quickly. He glanced towards Mason with one eyebrow raised slightly. "Looks like we're right on time, Great and Illustrious leader."

"There is no time to be on, you jack-ass."

"Then why were you getting your fucking panties in a bunch earlier?"

"You know very well why, now shut up and get going."

Porter shook his head loftily. "You are too damn sneaky for your own good sometimes, Mason."

"And you are too fucking clever for everyone's. We need to present our credentials. Stay back, don't get in front or be obvious, Porter. He might actually remember you from your freakish height, you know."

"Fuck, I forgot about that." Porter frowned absently. "Fuck fuck fuck."

"Yes, you said that already. Just don't draw attention. Most likely, he won't remember you, and you do look very different, especially with your beard on." Mason gestured the two of them to walk behind him and he handed the large canvas sack to James. "Just slouch a lot. I don't like this. Something feels wrong."

"Yeah, thanks, Mason."

"You're welcome. Now shut the hell up and stay quiet and in the background." Mason couldn't shake the feeling that somebody had known Porter and James would be buying diamonds. It was too clean, too neat. As they walked through the dusty sunbaked courtyard, he pondered who might have been behind this sort of thing. Somebody had tipped Emil off about the diamond broker. Mahmoud's hadn't been that big an operation and he shouldn't have been targeted on that exact day. It was possible that it was a coincidence. Mason didn't think so, though. Coincidences didn't often happen in this line of work.

Chapter 11

Mason drew himself up importantly as they neared the entrance. The two guards glanced at him and gestured them through. Mason ignored them completely. He walked through the opening as if he owned this house. People tended to defer to the ones who seemed to be in charge. Useful conceit.

The hall was long and had high ceilings. The floors were covered in expensive and deep carpets. It was pleasantly cool inside. Mason walked purposefully through the hall towards the back of the building. There were other voices coming from that area. Calmly, Mason assumed a serious, blank face. He couldn't show any emotion at all. Emil was the type who would be more impressed by a man who was more like a rock than one who was emotive. Besides, a poker face like that would help if they had to face the women in back.

The table that each group of men was going to was large, beautifully made and obviously expensive. Mason waited soberly with James and Porter right behind him. He didn't look around. He was in charge here, and he didn't deign look weak in front of anyone.

It took perhaps fifteen minutes for those in front to get done and go off wherever it was that they had to go. Mason was careful to not look curious. Porter and James would see what he needed to know. That was what they were there for. He had to lead this. To that end, he stepped up to the table carelessly.

There were three men sitting behind the table. They each had the white uniform of the Army. None had a keffiyeh. The one in the middle was the one in charge; that was easy for Mason to read. The other two must be bookkeepers or secretaries or something. It didn't much matter. He addressed only the one with power.

"I heard that you have some unique merchandise this sale. I am here to buy." He said abruptly.

The man nodded carefully. "Yes, yes, we do." He studied Mason closely. Mason stood impassive. Finally, the man said a bit hesitantly, "Are you from the Saud region?"

79

"Does it matter? I have the requirements. I think that is all you need." Mason did not want to give any information to this man. Information could be checked. It would be far too dangerous. "I said that you have unique merchandise. I have the means to purchase. What more do you need?"

"Nothing, sir. But you must concede that it seems odd for…"

Mason cut the comment off. "I concede nothing. If you have no interest in selling to me, I will take my slaves and find another market more amenable to me."

"Sir, please, I must confer with a superior."

"I suggest you do that as quickly as possible." Mason said drily. He looked over the head of the man, dismissing him. The man's cheeks flushed with anger or humiliation, but he didn't challenge Mason. Instead, he rang a small silver bell.

There was a twitching of the curtain, and another man stepped out. Porter shifted behind Mason. It wasn't Emil; it was one of the generals. They had to be more careful now.

"A thousand pardons, General! I need you to vouch for this buyer. He is not one who has been here before."

The general stared at the three of them for some moments, looking curious. Without looking at the men at the table, he directed a question at them. "Who are they?"

"I have no name, sir. They have heard of the, uh, uniqueness of this sale."

The general continued to stare at Mason. He seemed puzzled by something. "Are they not of the house of Saud?"

"They did not say, sir."

"Most curious." The general murmured to himself. "Very curious, indeed." Mason continued to stare back, his face impassive. He pretended like he knew they would be accepted and these were just formalities. The general finally spoke to Mason directly. "How did you come to be here?"

Mason maintained his direct look. He waited to answer, and then said slowly, "Who has not heard of this? I thought that the Army of the Almighty wanted this sort of information out. I grow tired of being questioned to no end, General. I sense that you are unwilling or unable to honor a sale. Did the Army not wish to make money?"

"Yes. Yes, that is true, however…"

The curtain parted and Emil himself came out. Mason heard James take a quick breath in, but that was the only outward sign he gave. Emil came up to the table.

"What appears to be keeping you, Usama? I wanted to go over the next week's campaigns with the whole staff." He said impatiently.

General Usama gestured to Mason. "This man and his slaves have come for the sale. We were attempting to make sure of them."

Mason looked at Emil haughtily. "I can give my validity in one word." He snapped his fingers to James and took the bag from him without taking his eyes off Emil. "Here." He untied the bag and upended it with a flourish. Emil and General Usama both stared greedily at the pile of uncut diamonds and gold coins. Mason allowed them to look for a few seconds. He tossed the bag negligently on top of the pile. "These are my credentials, gentlemen. Either accept them or don't; I am not accustomed to waiting, and I don't like being questioned. I grow weary of this; soon I shall become angry."

Emil took a few of the pieces of diamond and looked them over. "All right. Clear them. These credentials are acceptable." He nodded to Usama and they both left. The secretaries quickly weighed out the diamonds and counted the gold.

The man who had first addressed Mason took the paper the secretary handed him and glanced at it. "You have here an amount equal to about eight million rial, sir. We will hold this amount for you, and if you have a higher amount that you wish to bring with you to the sales tomorrow, you may. We will hold this as an advance, and as a deposit. If you do not bid, or do not win, we will return it to you."

Mason nodded shortly and gestured sharply to Porter. Porter quickly and obsequiously gathered it all back into the bag and tied it. He handed it to Mason and stepped back, his face carefully turned towards the ground. Mason didn't look at him. He took the bag and looked at it.

"I require a seal for this. I would not want to find anything missing from it."

"Yes, Sir! Have you a seal?"

"I do." Mason reached inside his tunic and removed a chain from his neck. It had a cylinder seal on it.

"Good, sir. Here." The man snapped his fingers at one of the scribes. The scribe reached under the table and removed a small box. It had a lead bar in it, and the man quickly heated it over a small lamp and clamped it around the bag.

Mason rolled his seal over the soft metal to leave the imprint. He nodded to the man. "Very good."

The scribe took the bag and left to another room with it. The man nodded to himself. "Would you care to inspect the merchandise now or later with the other buyers?"

Mason made a gesture with his hand as if he was shooing an irritating fly away. "Now, of course. I do not pay top prices to mingle with the unwashed infidels."

"Yes, sir. Hashim will show you the way." He clapped his hands together twice sharply and a soldier appeared quickly. "Your slaves are most welcome to stay here."

Mason bowed slightly. He turned and gestured imperiously to James and Porter. "Do as he tells you and stay here." Porter and James both bowed very low and moved to the wall. Mason turned back to his escort. "Lead on. I am impatient."

"Yes, sir. This way." The soldier turned at went through an arched doorway off the main hall. Mason followed, making careful observations as he went. The door led to another hallway, this one not as grand or showy. The ceiling was rough unpainted stucco and the walls were unadorned.

The hall was perhaps a hundred meters long. It ended in an impressively thick and padlocked door.

"Please wait, sir. I must signal the other guards." Hashim said as he tapped on the door a few times.

"Who is it?" Someone on the other side said loudly.

"Hashim. I am leading a buyer."

"Sir." There was a scraping of locks being drawn. The door swung open rather ponderously. It seemed quite heavy and rather well used, Mason noted bleakly.

"This way, sir." Hashim gestured and went through.

Chapter 12

The slave pens were hot and they stunk. Mason pitied any humans forced into shit-holes like this. No wonder the UN wanted to remove them from Emil's power. The ability to intimidate with these types of things was tremendous. Mason shrugged mentally. Emil was about to lose control of more than slaves.

The men were in one pen, the women as far as possible from them. No one returned Mason's looks, but he thought the women seemed disdainful. Good. Gabriella and Karen had been working their magic, then.

"Here, sir. Here are the last." Hashim said as they came to some isolated cells. These would be the highest interest, highest priced women. Mason looked in each cell. There were several young girls, some teenagers, and the last held Callie and Sienna. Mason did not linger over any. He merely noted that Sienna and Callie both were sleeping. They wouldn't know he had come, which was unfortunate in some ways. He wanted them reassured, but then again, they might act differently if they knew. Talk about a fucking catch-22.

Mason turned airily. "Very good. I will be here to bid tomorrow. Time?"

Hashim looked very confused. "Sir?"

"What time does bidding begin, idiot?" Mason said impatiently.

"The sale, it begins at 8:00."

Mason nodded once. "I shall go now."

When they returned to the main hall, there were several other groups waiting to be validated or to be escorted through the pens. Mason ignored them all. He was counting heavily on Porter and James to have watched. As he walked towards them, he did noticed at least two other tall men in the hall. Good. Porter wasn't going to be as conspicuous as they had thought. About time to catch a fucking break.

Mason snapped his fingers imperiously and Porter and James moved silently and swiftly in behind him. However, before they made it far, a voice Mason recognized stopped them. "Sir! A moment?"

Mason turned irritably. "What more?" He snapped.

Emil had come back out from the curtained room. He gestured Mason to a side door. Mason was curious about this; what did Emil want now? He had the money and Mason was sure that he hadn't recognized Porter or James. Even Sienna and Callie would be hard-pressed to recognize them. Mason nodded and moved to the room, Porter and James in tow. "What else is there?" He asked carefully.

Emil gestured him to an ornate side table with comfortable chairs. "I thought you might be interested in another option. Please, sit. We can have a small drink. Would your servants care for anything?"

Mason shrugged. "They would appreciate a drink, I am sure. I do not allow my slaves to be spoiled by frequent rewards, but this is a special occasion. It may seem presumptuous, but I consider it an early celebration in what I am sure I will acquire tomorrow."

Emil nodded in apparent agreement. "You are most correct; that is the way to best deal with slaves." He rang a small bell and a serving man appeared quietly after a few moments with a silver tray loaded with delicate cups and a silver pitcher. Emil poured four cups and relaxed back into his chair back. Mason sipped his drink very cautiously. It seemed to be some sort of black tea, chilled, with citrus flavors.

"This is very good. Thank you. Now, what did you wish to discuss?"

Emil sipped at his own cup briefly. "I had a proposition for you. You say you came expressly for this sale?"

Mason inclined his head. "I make no secret to my motivation."

"No, indeed. I think you are interested in the more unique merchandise that I have acquired?"

Mason nodded again. "I would think you have many such buyers."

"Perhaps not so many as one might expect. That is really beside the point. The reason I am asking is because I am trying to find the best way to get them on the block."

Mason waited. He wasn't totally sure how to handle this situation just yet and silence was a better ally than saying something fucking stupid.

Emil sipped more of his tea. He looked speculatively at Mason. "Do you think they would draw a better price together, or separately? We must both admit that they are a bit skinny and scrawny for what the buyers usually want."

"True, but they are going for a different skill set than these two might possess. Allow me to be frank. If I buy them, I will not be buying serving girls. I will be buying wives or concubines. They do not have to stand up to much physically for that purpose."

Emil nodded. "That is how they will be used, undoubtedly."

"As to selling them together? Well, I would not object to only having to bid once for both. I do not know if you will get a higher price that way. You might do best if they are up first however, when all the buyers have their money still. Those who wish to bid on those two may hold out for them, to conserve their reserves. The bidding may be lower on your other options if they are not first."

Emil considered that for some minutes. "Yes. Yes, you might be right. I think that you are right. They must be first. Those interested will not want to wait and will hold out until they are up. Excellent advice."

Mason took another sip to hide his own excitement. If they put Sienna and Callie up first, he would not have to go hunting for them after the UN busted the operation open. "Sir, if you put them up together, I will set an opening bid of two million rial. I mean to have them." He paused significantly. "Unless you might be willing to sell them now. I doubt that is the case, but I shall try my luck anyway."

Emil smiled. "Of course, you must try! However, I cannot honor that option. I shall open bids tomorrow at two million and we shall see! May Allah favor you tomorrow."

"Indeed we shall see. May I drink to your continued health?" Mason raised his cup slightly.

Emil smiled and inclined his head graciously. "Indeed you may. I wish you all the luck and grace of Allah tomorrow. I may not know your name or where you come from, but I sense a kindred spirit."

Mason sipped his cup, glad that Porter had trained him so well to hide a smile. Yeah, he thought, you and I are alike. We're both out to fuck someone over and we're both hiding our real intentions here. You must want something from me. Maybe it was the initial number to start bidding at; maybe it is to see if you could get an identity out of me. Whatever it was, I hope you think you got it. And then, I hope you never realize how close you were to death.

He and Emil continued to sip the tea, neither saying anything else. Mason continued to think about what Emil wanted. Even if the three of them never made it out of this building alive, the sting would go down tomorrow. The UN was moving in already. Whether he ever realized why or not, Emil was finished. Mason was glad that Porter hadn't moved to slice him up here and now. It must be taking great reserve on his part. Mason would have to thank him somehow, tangibly.

After perhaps fifteen minutes of chatter, Emil put his cup back on the silver tray. Mason followed suit, gesturing sharply for Porter and James to do likewise. Emil smiled as they moved to obey.

"You have trained your servants well. If you win these women, Allah will bless you plentifully."

"I hope so. I do not appreciate servants who do not perform exactly as I wish. It demonstrates a lack of character."

Emil nodded. "You are right, of course. And it demonstrates weakness in the owner. Weakness cannot be permitted to exist. Allah calls us to be the strong and the rulers."

"All rulers should be strong, whether they rule domestically or publicly."

"You are a voice of reason amid so much babbling. I wish you luck tomorrow. Until then." Emil bowed slightly.

Mason stood and bowed as well. He left the room with Porter and James.

Chapter 13

Once they were outside, Porter heaved a huge sigh of relief. "Goddamn fucking painful!" He rolled his shoulders back a few times, standing to his full height again.

Mason smiled slightly. "Your own fucking fault."

"Shut up."

"I know it hurts to stoop. And it must be a fucking pain with your side being the way it is. You did very well at not killing Emil. I am sorry to have to tempt you with it."

Porter shrugged. "It wasn't time yet. You did a fucking good job being vague. You also did a good job leading him to put the women up first."

"It's not hard to tell people what they want to hear, you know. Especially a fucking messed-up egotistical bastard like that."

"Did you see them?" James asked eagerly. It was obvious he was not referring to Emil.

"Yes. Both were asleep." Mason hesitated, looking at James, then said, "James, I am not trying to tell you what to do or anything but if you are this emotionally involved, you might as well fucking ask her to marry you and get it the fuck over with. Women like Callie deserve to be won, not lead along for fucking forever."

"I know, Mason. My parents don't mind, but they belong to the high society crowd. I am not sure Callie wants in on that."

"Why not let her decide that? Just give her the option."

Porter smiled. "Besides, think of how much she would shake that snotty crowd up."

James also smiled. "I have, many times. I don't want her to think she needs to change for them, though. And I should probably ask her parents first. They might try to change her mind."

"After this vacation, she won't change for anybody. Trust me."

"Vacation. Right."

"It is. Being captured is always very invigorating. The zest keeps you young and on your toes."

88

"And you would know this, of course."

"Well, shit yes, James. I have lost count of how many times I fucked something up and was in so fucking deep Mason had to come for me." Porter said calmly. "Sometimes, I think half the fucking mission is Mason trying to fucking bail me out or fucking smooth over my mistakes."

Mason sighed. "Porter, shut the fuck up. You are victim-stancing and projecting. Again!"

"I know. I am sorry. I meant to be exaggerating for comedic effect."

"Well, do you believe what you said?"

"Uh." Porter thought for a few moments. "Now that you mention it: no, Mason, I don't. I know you do much more than wait around breathlessly for me to fuck up. I know that I do things correctly much more often. Still gives me gray hair every time, though. This last one must have added pounds of it. I may have to start dying my hair."

"Good. About fucking time. And leave your hair the fuck alone. Accept who you are, in all fucking ways."

"Anyway, James," Porter turned back to James, "I am offering here and now to make the rings for Callie and if you want one too, should you wish to accept that."

James stared at Porter. "You would do that for us?" He sounded completely incredulous.

"Shit, James. Of course I would. Why are you so surprised? I like doing things for friends."

"Well, I don't know. You are the best. I'm not just saying that, either. You really are the best. I thought maybe, I don't know, we were below you, or something. You have so many famous people who want your designs. I guess I thought you wouldn't want to do something this low. I mean, we're nobody." James mumbled. He still clearly thought he was walking in Porter's shadow.

"And you think I have problems, Mason? I hate when people act all surprised that I want to do things for friends! Doesn't anybody give me any fucking credit?" Porter said in a despairing voice. Mason smiled.

89

Porter shook his head. "Yes, I will do it. I want to do it. You make far too much of status, James, and you really need to get the fuck over it. I would much rather design for somebody I know and love than some air-headed celebrity who will just throw it into some damn box and forget about it. Will you let me?"

James nodded mutely.

"Good. Glad that is fucking decided. Best compliment I have ever received was from Juan refusing to buy one of our designs because he knew it would be thrown away, James. That means much more than fucking money or inflated ego or fucking stature. It shows that he values us for more than gold. You and your status hang-ups blind you sometimes. Juan refused to buy any designs you did, you know." He turned to Mason. "Mason, did you notice if Sienna's rings were gone? I just sort of assumed they would be."

Mason nodded. "They are. All her jewelry is gone; Callie's, too. Sorry, Porter. We all knew your designs are worth too much for Emil to leave them. You're too much a fucking genius for your own damn good that way."

Porter shrugged. "Then I will make more."

"I'm glad you aren't too upset by that."

"Yeah, well, it wouldn't do any good to be going to fucking pieces over something that can be remedied fairly easily."

"I know that; I am just glad you do, too. Took you fucking long enough."

"You know, Dr. Mitchel never says shit like that."

"I'm not fucking Dr. Mitchel. I am your fucking friend and I get to make fucking observations like that because of it."

James nodded seriously. "I sincerely hope you are not fucking Dr. Mitchel. That sort of thing really should be kept separate from the office environment."

Mason started laughing.

Back at the safe house, Porter started getting some food ready and Mason started sketching things out for his planning. James sat at the table quietly. Once Mason had a general outline, he put his notebook aside and said loudly to Porter, "And now you're going to deal us a hand or twenty. We have until eight tomorrow morning to calm down before this all goes to Hell again."

"A hand of what game?"

"Who the fuck cares? I will be back within the hour and you had better have food and a game ready."

Porter turned suspiciously. "Where the fuck are you going?"

Mason smiled impishly. "I have to let the UN brigade know what to expect."

"That can't be all."

"You'll just have to wait to find out about the rest, Porter."

Porter looked disgusted. He turned back to the counter. "You know I hate that, Mason. Drives me fucking nuts when Juan does it."

"Shit, Porter, why do you think I do it too?" Mason left, chuckling to himself. He didn't always get to catch Porter by surprise, and it was a small triumph when he could.

The small, grubby shop he'd seen was off the main street slightly. Mason was observant enough to know what it was, so he glanced around to make sure no one was paying him any attention before he slipped in.

The man inside glanced up quickly. Mason did not make direct eye-contact, picked up a dusty and nondescript bottle with no label and a significant amount of liquid in it, handed some coins over and left. All this was done without any significant looks. Mason would be unable to describe the man inside, and he would be unable to describe Mason. Win-win. He again made sure no one was interested in him.

The UN brigade was housed on base, but the commander was in a safe house across town. Mason quickly relayed the time and place the sale would be happening. "If you can, please try to hit it as close to the opening as you can. The high-interest sales are going to be first, and potential buyers who lose out will start to leave after that."

"All right. How do you know those will be first?"

"I helped Emil come to the idea in conversation."

The captain laughed. "That must have taken some finesse."

"A little, yes, but I have experience with that sort of thing. We'll see you tomorrow then?"

"Yes, Sir.""

"Wait until my team member gives you a signal. He is by far the biggest man in that place. He'll stand in the doorway and raise and lower his weapon three times significantly. He will then stand aside and make sure all the guards are out of commission. You should not be impeded in getting in."

"Very good, Sir. The less fighting we have to do the more likely we are of success."

Mason nodded and left the safe house to return to Porter and James, his bootleg bottle safely tucked up under his robes.

On the way back, he stopped at an open air market and bought some dates, figs and nuts. Porter would probably do something amazing with them. Besides, Mason liked dates, figs and nuts. He was buying so he got to choose. One of the stalls had slabs of lamb, and he also grabbed more flat bread and the apricot spread Porter was so fond of.

By the time he was back, Porter had produced some fantastic eggs, a savory yoghurt dip, and the ubiquitous flatbread. "You know, Mason, if you want real food, you better get me some fucking real shit to start with." Porter grumbled.

"Oh, like this shit?" Mason casually reached into the bag he carried and pulled out the various purchases.

"Hell yes!" Porter smiled enthusiastically, already cooking it all in his head. "Give me another half hour, and then we can eat like kings and play games all fucking night."

"An offer like that is impossible to turn down, you know." Mason laughed. He sat down near James. "So, James, my boy; what can I get you and Callie for your impending nuptials?"

James smiled. "Aren't you being rather premature, Dr. Briggs? I haven't rescued her yet, let alone asked her."

Mason gestured with one hand expansively. "I don't give a flying fuck about minor details like that."

"Minor?!" James laughed out loud. "You must be joking!"

"He is." Porter said absently without turning. "He is feeling fucking proud of himself, so he is more obnoxious than usual."

"I beg your damn pardon, I am not." Mason protested.

"You may not have my damn pardon and you are so."

"Whatever. Like you are the fucking picture of moderation."

"Takes one to know one."

"That's not fucking true and you know it."

"Whatever." Porter shrugged and gave up the argument. "It sounded good."

Mason snorted and also dropped the topic. "Anyway, James, what do you want?"

James smiled again. "I don't know, Mason. I honestly am freaked out a little about even asking her. What if she says 'no'?"

"Well, that is always a possibility, but then, Porter called us and asked us to come. He knew we could have said 'no', but he had to ask anyway. We each had to choose to say 'yes'. He had faith in us all, you know. Sometimes, we all have to have some faith."

"What, in God?"

"If that's where you think it should be." Mason shrugged. "Porter definitely has faith in God. I do, too, when it comes down to it. Somebody has to care about us, because there is too much to say everything happens by chance. I can't accept the idea of chaos."

"No, me neither, now that you mention it. Chaos would mean that there are no principles that hold true, and I think there are some, especially when it comes to beauty."

Mason nodded. "I agree with you. Beauty is ruled by something outside our own perceptions of it. That's why Porter's rings are better than the ones you get out of a bubblegum machine."

"Be fucking expensive bubblegum." Porter noted.

"So, Porter, why do you believe?" James asked interestedly.

Porter looked out the small window distractedly. He did that when he was thinking hard about something, Mason had noticed. He'd acquired the habit from Sienna. "Well, James, once a very beautiful young lady told me that she had to believe. That it was something she could not do without, like it was part of who she was, a part of her very nature. I think it's the same with me. I tried to run away from it, but it was always there, waiting for me to hit bottom. And when I did, like a ton of fucking bricks, it was the only thing waiting to take my back up. Faith is like that for me. I think it makes everything bearable. It's like a lantern beckoning in the darkness. There's nothing logical or even fucking rational in it." He shrugged and looked back at what he was doing. "Anyway, without it I would have fucking blown my brains out many years ago. And after the last few set-backs, it has kept me from becoming manic-depressive. I tried to drink it away, but I couldn't. And then Mason had his doctors fucking take that away. It's all I have left. So there you go. Happy shit from me to bring all the conversation up."

"But didn't you have friends to help you? Before, I mean."

"Friends? Me? You must be fucking joking, James. Having friends means letting people get to know you. I wasn't capable of that."

"Well, then, how did you meet up with Dr. Briggs? I thought you were friends?"

"We are now, but it was not until much later, James. I met Mason when he offered me a mission. He had seen me win some stupid street game to get the money back for some lady. She'd been sucked into one of those shell games. You know the type. Anyway, I got her money back, and I was done, but Mason cornered me and talked me up something fierce. Said he needed someone with my skills. You know how he can lay on the snow-job when he wants something. So I agreed to get him to go away. He held me to it, though. I was too fucking introverted to think he would remember me. I thought no one saw me as a person. I wasn't worth seeing. Too fucked up. That was one of my darkest periods. It's fucking hard to come to realize people might actually like me as I am. Took fucking years."

"Wow. I would have never guessed. How did you end up as

friends then?"

Mason smiled. "Well, you must admit that Porter is always fucking exciting and fun to be around. Besides, he used to get roaring smashed in those days, so he talked a lot more when he was in that state. I knew more of the real Porter than he thought. I liked that one better than the façade he puts up anyway. One of them was one helluva good guy, and one was a loser because it was a one-dimensional closed person."

Porter was searing the lamb over the stove. He didn't say anything to Mason's observations. Mason wasn't even totally sure he'd heard. Probably. Porter rarely missed shit like this.

In a few minutes, he brought the smoking roast to the table with the rest of the food. The lamb had been stuffed with dates. It was just as amazing as Mason had thought it would be.

"Oh, one other thing." Mason snapped his fingers as if he had just remembered. "Here. We'll need some glasses or cups. That's my contribution to the festivities. Now get your fucking cards out. You better fucking contribute too." He put the bottle on the table.

Porter looked at the bottle with one eyebrow raised slightly. He grinned. "You never cease to amaze me, Mason. I thought this was illegal."

Mason shrugged nonchalantly and took a fig. "Oh, it is. There's always a way around any law though, especially if one wants to make a fucking profit. I can't guarantee the quality."

"Who fucking cares? It can't be as bad as the pig slop we had in Chile."

"Nor the piss-drink we had in Thailand."

Porter shuddered. "Oh, God! I had forgotten that shit."

"Well, I haven't. So this probably isn't that bad."

"Good. You pour. I have the cards right here." And as if by magic flourish, there was a deck in his hands.

Mason shook his head. "I never can catch you doing that."

"Practice, Mason. Besides, it wouldn't be nearly as fun if you could. I keep practicing it just so you won't."

"Probably true. You gonna deal, or you gonna sit there looking fucking pleased with yourself?"

"Ready to lose, ladies?"

"Fuck you, Porter. Deal and shut up."

"Your fucking funeral." Porter smiled and shuffled professionally. "By the way, Mason, what the hell has been bugging you?"

Mason picked up his cards and looked them over. "I'm not sure, Porter. I just feel like the coincidences are piling up too fucking fast. No one should have targeted Mahmoud; he's not a big enough buyer. If all they wanted was diamonds, there are lots of safer and quicker ways to get them than a chancy robbery. No one should have targeted the exact time you two would be there. No one should have shot you two. All of that is a great way to get international scrutiny on an operation, and not the favorable kind. Just feels wrong, like this fucking hand you dealt. What the hell? This sucks worse than what you usually slough off on me."

"Serves you right, bitch. We are still going in tomorrow, despite all your misgivings, right?"

"Hell yes. Take care of one fucking problem at a time."

"Good. That's what I want to hear. Ante up, boys."

Part II

Chapter 14

Callie was terrified; she and Sienna had been forced out of the room so fast she didn't see if James was even alive still. Sienna had made it to Porter, but Callie had been so shocked and frightened that she was paralyzed. James was back in that room, covered in blood, possibly dead, and she and Sienna were being half-carried out of the building. Even if she had known how to fight, it would have been useless. There were too many men around her. They all had large rifles, although Callie had no idea what types they were. She figured it likely that they would not hesitate to shoot her down if she tried anything. Not that she could; she had no experience with this sort of thing.

If it had been a social gathering in Upper Manhattan or something like that, she would have been able to negotiate it all fairly well. None of that training would help her here, except maybe the mental ability to remain composed. She would have to wrap that dignity around herself and wear it like armor. It was her only defense to employ. Nothing in finishing school or any of her previous life had prepared her for this sort of situation.

If her old friends could only see her now! They would never recognize her, and even if they had, they would have been aghast. No true lady would be in such a false situation. She could almost hear them whispering softly about it and pasting bright plastic smiles on. They would console her with empty murmurs and look at her with judgmental eyes.

Sienna stumbled against her and Callie forced herself back into the present. It would not do to be imagining things that hadn't happened. She sternly gave herself a mental shake. She could not be playing this game where she wrapped herself in fantasy. Sienna needed her to be here, now. She had to do it. She had failed to help James; she could not let Sienna down.

Callie put her arm around Sienna and steadied her. Sienna looked shaken; there was blood all over her dress and arms. It was Porter's blood. She'd been married less than ten hours and then this had happened. Callie shuddered to herself. She simply couldn't imagine that.

The men around them shoved them into the back of large transport truck. Callie thought it looked like the types of canvas-covered troop transports she'd seen back in the United States. There were benches on either side and there were two men already in there. They forced Callie and Sienna onto the end seats, closest to the open back, and pointed rifles at them.

Callie was scared by all this. She looked at Sienna for an idea of what to do. Sienna sat very straight looking like she was upset. She did wink at Callie though. Maybe Callie wasn't doing too badly after all.

Emil, the one who seemed to be in charge, came striding out of the building. He looked very pleased about something, Callie thought. She hoped that he hadn't checked on Porter and James and made sure they were dead. Before she could register what he was doing, he had come to the back of the truck and was examining them with as little interest and emotion as if they were blocks of wood. He grasped her arm perfunctorily and glanced at her bracelet. It had been a gift from James. She knew he had worked a long time on it and she loved it for that more than its technical execution.

Emil also looked Sienna over, then he smiled. "Remove their jewelry. It will be worth much on the market, more than all the diamonds we have come into possession of." He said as he turned away. One of the other soldiers wretched Sienna's rings and bracelet off and took Callie's bracelet, as well as her gold chain necklace and her watch. Even though she knew it would do no good, Callie tried to keep out of reach of the soldier.

He impassively pulled her arm up behind her excruciatingly. Callie cried, but they took her bracelet anyway. With a look of contempt, the soldier shoved her back onto her bench. Callie cradled her arm and cried. She couldn't stop. They had taken her last link to James. He might be dead and she now had no physical way to remind herself of him. Another soldier came and tied her wrists together in front of her with as little interest as Emil had shown.

She felt empty and afraid, so she cried and cried. She didn't notice the truck starting until the lurching of it moving almost threw her out of the back. One of the soldiers had to grab her shoulder. He looked disgusted and let go quickly. He turned away from her dismissively as soon as he could.

Callie had never felt so isolated and alone before. She had never been somewhere where she wasn't worth human compassion before. She felt herself going back into her fantasy world. She often went there when she was in a stressful situation. It sometimes helped her to remove herself from her surroundings by retreating to a world she controlled.

Almost on cue, she seemed to see Mason Briggs striding into her vision and speaking to her sharply. "Get out of here, Callie! You can day-dream later! I need you right now!"

She jerked herself awake. She even caught herself about to apologize. How ridiculous. Maybe she was going crazy under the strain. Wearily, she looked out the back of the truck. The road was not good and they were jostled together by the potholes and rough drive. Callie was hampered by her hands being tied. She couldn't steady herself, and the soldiers seemed annoyed about having to help her. She mumbled something about being sorry but no one answered or acknowledged that she had said anything. Callie started to feel numb about it all. She even wondered if she had really lived here forever and was only now waking up to the fact. Time stopped meaning anything. There was only now, this empty moment.

She slipped into a twilight sort of place. Nothing she saw really registered. She didn't even feel like herself anymore. The landscape was rocky and barren, the sunlight so bright it bleached all color out of the rocks. Callie would never be able to tell the way they were being taken; she knew she would be useless out in that desert by herself. She was already confused about direction. The sun beat mercilessly outside the truck. She watched the horizon shimmering and shivering from heat and became entranced by the shifting lines. It was as if even the earth, so solid and eternally real, no longer had set boundaries anymore. Everything began to waver. Nothing was firm, nothing was set.

Everything could change at whim. It could all wink out of existence in a second.

Again, she mentally heard Mason say impatiently, "Wake up!" and she struggled to focus.

The men didn't talk to her or Sienna. In fact, they hardly spoke to each other. Gradually, Callie began to awaken again. She noticed something she hadn't noticed before: the men were afraid of something. She began to see that they glanced around furtively and once or twice hunched as if expecting a blow. At first she assumed they were afraid of being followed and caught. However, a chance comment and sharp rebuttal made her change her mind. They were afraid of Emil. She knew she was right, even as she struggled to justify her conclusions.

Callie began to think about that idea. If they were afraid of him, why would they follow him? There must be some reason. The more she considered it, the more her curiosity grew. Finally, she had something outside herself to pull her away from the dangerous place she had been. Almost desperately, she began to analyze everything the men said, how they acted, everything she could observe. She knew her sanity depended on it, but she didn't know why.

"We cannot be caught with them." One man grumbled.

"Emil cares not." Another said softly.

"No, and it matters not." A third man said sharply. Even though he spoke the loudest, he still spoke too softly for his voice to carry far. "We do as he orders."

The first man shook his head very slightly. "We do as he orders and we bleed our own blood."

"It matters not." The third said again and the conversation ceased for time. Callie noticed that the other men in the truck had nodded or showed other signs of assent to what the first one had said. These men were fighting a war for a man they feared. Why would they do that? What gain overrode their revulsion? Or perhaps what fear?

"I heard Emil wants it spread." A man rasped.

"He does. This sale will bring much money." Another

acknowledged.

"It will bring much blood." The first man with the raspy voice countered. "They cannot leave this as it stands. They will hunt us like snakes."

"We shall all pay for the sins of Emil." Another man said morbidly.

"It is true. Unless they make Emil pay his own sins."

"No one will. When they fail he will butcher them like sheep."

"Yes. Like the fourth." Several of the men shuddered or looked down quickly. Again, there was a pause. By now, Callie was actively curious. She had always been attracted to trying to figure out what motivated peoples' actions. She tried to appear uninterested even as she strained her ears for the next time they spoke. She concentrated so hard, she felt like her ears physically turned and rotated, like a cat's.

Because she was so focused, she didn't notice at first that they had slowed. The truck had come to a city or town and was driving between tall buildings on narrow streets. The jolting of the truck hadn't changed much, but it had slowed significantly.

It was the sound of animals that alerted her to the change. That, and the smell of food. Suddenly, Callie was ravenously hungry. Her stomach made some protesting noises that no one could fail to hear. One of the men laughed and said something in another language. Two others nodded. Callie decided she didn't care. She was coming out of that numb state she'd been in. Focusing on the men had helped, and now she caught Sienna's eye. Sienna looked calm, but Callie knew her well and saw that she was very upset still. Callie had to be strong for Sienna's sake. She straightened herself as best she could on the hard bench and mentally composed herself.

It was very possible that James and Porter were dead or incapacitated. She had to face it, and she had to get beyond it. That meant she had to look for ways to act on her own. It was a hard thought for her: it was difficult to think that she might never be rescued. It was difficult to consider that she might have to rescue herself. It was hard to think that she could only rely on herself, especially since she had no experiences like this.

It didn't much matter. There were no other options that she would accept.

From now on, it was Sienna and her against this army, and she was going to have to be up for it.

Chapter 15

The truck pulled to a shuddering halt somewhere. There was a cacophony of noise that burst into Callie's ears. The truck's engine and creaking had been so persistent that she had almost gotten used to it, and when it ceased, the outside noise was much more evident.

Then the truck gave another lurch forward and continued on. Callie struggled to stay on her seat, and again the disgusted soldier had to steady her.

She wasn't stupid and she knew that many looked down on women as almost subhuman. She'd heard James and Porter discussing it idly in the store once or twice. From the reactions of these soldiers, she figured they were definitely in that category. She deliberately kept her eyes down to not provoke anything she didn't have to. Meekness and outward subservience were probably her best course of action right now, at least until she figured out how she should act. It couldn't hurt to be too cautious at first.

The truck rumbled on through streets and alleys. Finally, after what seemed like a long time, it stopped and the engine was quiet. The men began to stand and move around. Callie figured they were at some destination but she wasn't sure if she was supposed to get up. While she considered it, Callie glanced out the back of the truck. There were some other men in uniforms like the soldiers in the back. They looked to be lounging around.

It was getting close to evening, and Callie hadn't eaten in hours. Her stomach protested again loudly. Callie wished she could make it stop doing that. It was hard to remain inconspicuous when she kept having growling noises come from her stomach. The men in the truck laughed again. One of them nudged another. "We need to feed that beast."

The other laughed. "It roars!"

Callie kept her head down and tried to keep her face as blank as she could even as her cheeks burned. She desperately wished she had learned to play more cards and had a better poker face. There was nothing for it now, of course. The men were getting out of the truck even as she thought about it. She didn't get up or give any hint that she noticed them.

Once, she snuck a look across at Sienna. She had her face down, too. Callie felt a little surer of herself. If Sienna was doing the same thing, perhaps she wasn't doing anything too wrong yet.

The men were all outside the truck now. They stood around as if waiting for something although Callie wasn't sure what it might be.

"What do we do?" She heard one of the soldiers ask softly. It seemed that she wasn't the only one who had no idea. The soldiers kept glancing around. This must be a new situation for them too. Of course! Callie remembered that Emil had said something about this being a headline-grab. Headlines could only be grabbed by something new or different, so this whole thing must be new for everyone.

"We have to wait for Emil. These are special." Someone outside replied.

So they would have to wait. Callie knew she would get more nervous the longer it would take. The men outside continued to talk amongst themselves and seemed to not be paying a great deal of attention to them, so Callie thought she would be okay trying to talk to Sienna.

She flicked her hand towards Sienna. Sienna nodded very slightly. She'd seen her.

"What do we do?" Callie whispered as quietly as she could. A little guidance wouldn't hurt and she seriously needed some.

"We wait. Don't make eye contact and speak only when spoken to."

"Okay." Callie knew she shouldn't tempt fate and ask too many questions right now even though she felt so badly out-of-place. Maybe that wouldn't be too unfortunate for her. Hopefully if she seemed uncomfortable, the soldiers would be more willing to ignore her. Callie somehow knew that if they ignored her that she was safer than if they were focused on her. Suddenly, Callie found herself wishing she had boring hair instead of the light red she liked so much. There were few enough redheads in the US. Here she would stand out like a candle in a dark room. Sienna's light brown would, too. It would be hard to be invisible.

And still they waited. Callie was tired, both from the heat, probably from dehydration, and from sitting so long. After perhaps half an hour, Emil materialized and gave some orders that had to do with water and food.

One of the soldiers climbed up and jerked her to her feet, and Callie immediately stumbled. Her legs had gone numb. The soldier shoved her out of the back of the truck and into the arms of the other soldiers standing outside. They held her up until she could stand on her own, then of course they let go as quickly as possible.

Sienna was also thrown out of the back. Callie thought she looked very pale, and she had trouble standing up. Callie quickly moved beside her.

"Lean on me, Sienna." She whispered softly.

Sienna smiled very wanly in response and seemed to almost wilt against her. The soldiers who were standing in the courtyard hurriedly brought some leather bags of water.

Emil nodded to the two women. "Drink. You will need it. Then drink more."

Callie opened her mouth and drank obediently. Sienna did it mechanically. The water splashed down her face and neck, but she didn't seem to notice. Then Callie drank more. Sienna refused. Callie was worried about her friend. It was obvious that Sienna was suffering.

"Bring them food, but not too much at first. We don't have time to fatten them up for the sale. It will lower the value significantly, but there is nothing for it. Pity." Several men nodded. Callie almost smiled at the difference between expectations here and back home. In the US, it was more attractive to be slender. Here, they wanted plump women. Oh well. Callie couldn't do anything about it, and Sienna was already refusing to drink. Callie was fairly sure that she wouldn't eat, either. Not that Callie could blame her. If she'd just gotten married after years of being with someone and then been widowed so fast, she was pretty sure she'd go insane. She had to keep Sienna from doing exactly that. Callie needed her.

Besides, there was no guarantee that James and Porter were actually dead. And if they weren't dead, perhaps they had gotten word to Mason. Hope started to fill Callie. Careful, she cautioned herself. All sorts of things could get in the way. Mason might very well not know, and if he did, he might not know where they were, and even if he knew all that, it might not be possible to get them out. It didn't matter; once she'd thought about it, the hope flared in her. She had always been the type of the person who looked for the positive side of things anyway.

The slop the soldiers brought was unappetizing, but Callie ate some anyway. If healthy food didn't taste good, then this food was very healthy, she thought. Sienna ate only a bite or two. The soldiers presented more water and Callie obediently drank. She felt a little like a new baby bird or something. Sienna took a small amount.

Emil was talking to some other soldier the whole time. Callie thought this man looked like he was in control of something. Maybe it was one of Emil's generals or whatever they had here. Although she was more able to focus, Callie still was having trouble caring. She just couldn't bring herself to find out more. Instead, she stared at a spot on the cracked pavement. The talking around her ebbed and flowed, and she couldn't follow any of it. Finally, it was just too much and she felt the entire world grow fuzzy and indistinct. It seemed like her ears were stuffed with cotton. She couldn't hear correctly. Wearily, she tried to focus her eyes on something else, but it was just too much effort. Her legs felt like lead, her arms wouldn't move. What was happening? She closed her eyes to try and make them work.

Chapter 16

Callie seemed to be hearing James saying something. It was warm and he was saying something. She should pay attention. There were green trees and they were beside some lake somewhere. Callie felt herself turn, but then it all started to dissolve like a dream. Curiously, she watched everything melt back into the sun-baked courtyard in Morocco. She was lying on the ground. How had she gotten there? This was ridiculous. She was haunted by the feeling that she had just been somewhere else and the tenuous connection with reality created dissonance.

Callie struggled to move herself and stand up. She was far too weak. Her arms trembled uncontrollably and she couldn't get up. Sienna had been leaning on her, she remembered. Guiltily, Callie realized that she had also fallen and was kneeling beside her.

"Oh, Sienna, I am sorry. I didn't mean to pull you over. Or whatever I did. What happened?" Callie mumbled. She was still struggling mightily to rise.

Sienna smiled slightly. "My dear, you passed out. You were only out for a few seconds."

"Oh." Callie still felt confused.

Rough hands grabbed her and stood her up. Her knees wouldn't straighten, though, so the soldier had to keep holding her up.

"You idiots!" A man's voice was berating someone. With a rush, Callie remembered where she was and what had happened. "They must get out of this sun! Neither of them is very robust. Give them more water and then get them into the special cells."

The soldier holding Callie up grabbed her hair and pulled her head back as the soldier with the water approached. Callie drank as quickly as she could but the man poured too fast and she choked, spraying water as she gagged.

"Stop! She has to be alive!" Emil shouted.

The soldier backed away, terrified that he might be blamed for a mistake. Callie finally got all the water out of her lungs. The coughing left her even weaker. Sienna had drunk only a little, again. Emil watched anxiously, although Callie felt sure that he was interested only in if his merchandise was damaged. Once he felt sure that they would survive, he gestured sharply and the soldier holding Callie tried to direct her towards a building.

She was far too weak to walk on her own. The building might as well have been across town. Another soldier quickly slung his automatic rifle to his back and held her other shoulder. Between the two of them, Callie was forcefully carried to a yawning arched doorway.

It was noticeably cooler inside. There weren't any windows, and the sun couldn't reach the interior of the building with its baking heat. Callie tried to take active interest in her surroundings but she couldn't manage. It was too much for her. She still trembled and her stomach threatened to let everything she had just taken in come back up.

The passage they were in was long and dark. That was all Callie registered before they were at some door, and there were some words exchanged. A rattling sound of locks being opened focused Callie back into reality. The door swung open ponderously. It must be heavy and thick. Inside, it was hot and the air was close. It still was cooler than outside. The two soldiers carrying her passed through the doorway and into a long room full of cell-like rooms. Some were quite large, but the soldiers passed these by quickly and Callie couldn't see anything distinct.

They halted by a door, farthest from the one they'd entered through. One of the soldiers jerked his head impatiently and the one who had followed them from the door hurried to open it. The door was metal and had a barred window. Callie thought it looked a lot like a prison door.

Inside, there were two narrow cots. The floor was strewn with straw and was stone beneath. The walls were rough stone and looked totally solid. The soldiers supporting her pushed her to the cot on the right and turned away dismissively. Sienna was dumped with as little ceremony on the left cot. The door shut with a harsh clanging noise. Somehow, the noise made Callie more afraid than even the gunfire had. She hadn't really registered the gunfire; it had happened so quickly and everything that followed had been too fast for her to register properly. The door was immediately real. She was trapped and helpless except for Sienna. It was a terrible feeling.

The soldiers stood outside the cell talking softly for a while. Once they were gone, Callie looked across at Sienna.

"What should we do, Sienna?"

Sienna sighed and let her head fall back to the wall behind her. She drew her knees up to her chest, looking like she was trying to reassure herself of safety. "We have to wait and see what happens now. Porter wasn't dead when we left. It is possible that he got a call off to someone. It's our best chance now."

"And... and if he didn't?" Callie ventured.

"Then, my dear, we are going to be sold into someone's harem or household. Our best hope then is that we go together, and that we escape together."

Callie nodded slowly. "I'm sorry, Sienna. I'm just really scared. I don't have any idea of what I should do."

Sienna smiled weakly. "No, neither do I."

"You... you don't?"

"Of course not, Callie. I've not been in this type situation before."

"No, I didn't mean that. It's just that you have been so many places and done so much. It came out wrong."

"Don't apologize. I understand what you mean. The thing you must remember is that those other times and places, Mason was planning what happened and the other men were there to make it safe. We don't have either, unless Porter managed to not die and got a call to Mason off. We can't count on that though."

Callie shook her head. This was not a good place to be.

Sienna closed her eyes wearily. "If Porter and James are alive, they will come for us. I just don't know what to do to make that easier for them. And I don't even know if they are still alive. Porter was, but he was bleeding heavily. James was at least unconscious. They don't know where we are, they don't know how to get in or out. And they don't know when this sale is happening."

Callie started to cry. It was so hopeless and hard.

Sienna sighed. "Oh, Callie, I am sorry. I didn't mean to be so fucking blunt. Nothing is so black that it can't be made lighter."

"How, Sienna?" Callie wailed. "How can this be lighter? We're going to be sold and.. and... I don't even know what!"

Sienna nodded. "You're right. But we are alive, my dear. We are both still thinking. I know crying is natural. Don't be afraid of it, but don't let it get the best of you, either. I envy you, you know."

"What? Why?"

"Because I can't cry, not yet. I need to, but I cannot. I am too numb still."

"Is that a bad thing?"

Sienna smiled wryly. "It will be, if it bursts out of me in an inappropriate time and place. But come, my dear. Cry. Let it out. Wash yourself in tears. You may have to be the strong one if I cannot. If James and Porter are alive, they will come for us, someday. If they are not, Mason will hear of it sometime and he will come. We must be ready. I may not be able to help, so you may have to do it all. Let your grief run over and pass. And then, if you are inclined towards religious attitudes, pray for me, so that mine might come out, too. This is dangerous for me."

Callie didn't really understand, but she felt better all the same. She stood up and walked unsteadily over to sit beside Sienna. She leaned on her shoulder and cried.

It seemed like it took a long time for her to stop. There was no way to know for certain. Time meant next to nothing. Sienna still sat, still and stone-faced. She seemed as distant as the moon.

"Sienna?" Callie ventured at last.

Sienna closed her eyes and sighed. "Yes?"

"Are you going to be all right?"

"I don't know. I am not okay yet."

"Oh." Callie was quiet for a minute or two. She wanted to help Sienna, but she didn't know how. After a little while, she tried again. "Is there anything I can do for you?"

"Oh, my dear Callie, I wish there were! I don't know!" Sienna said softly. "We'll just have to see what happens. I think I need to sleep, though. You do, too. Maybe it will pass."

"I hope so."

"I do, too."

Callie was hardly reassured, but she was lost for anything else to do. Perhaps instinctively, she knew that Sienna was suffering and had tried to push it away. Callie didn't know what she could do to help, though. Sienna's belief that Mason would find them sometime was a hopeful one. Even though she didn't know if he knew yet, she couldn't shake the idea that Mason would be able to rescue them. Hope started to grow in her again. Somehow, the feeling that people cared about her and would come for her made her feel a bit calmer. That, and crying had helped, too. Mourning James had made her face it a little better.

Callie was not foolish and she knew she probably wasn't completely better, not yet. She was able to face the idea now. It hurt to think she might never see James again, and she was very upset even considering it, but she could face it. It was an important step. She knew it was.

She'd never been religious before, but Callie drifted off to sleep desperately murmuring. They were prayers remembered from long ago and she felt like she needed them now.

Chapter 17

It was some time later when Callie woke up. At first, she was confused by her surroundings. After a few seconds, she remembered where she was and how she'd ended up there. It was still a bit strange. She felt like the world was playing a joke on her and would sweep the entire cell away with in a big reveal. It didn't happen, of course, but the dissonance still remained.

Perhaps it was the oddness of the situation. Because she was unsure of herself, she was uncertain of the reality of the situation. Whatever the reason, she was nagged by a feeling that something was incorrect, somewhere.

Sienna still slept. Callie stood up stiffly and walked from one end of the small cell to the other. It took twelve steps to get from the door to the wall opposite.

Twelve steps.

She walked back and forth a few times, trying to settle her thoughts and emotions.

Twelve steps, turn. Twelve steps, turn.

James might be dead. She couldn't count on him rescuing her. Turn.

Sienna was slipping into listlessness. She couldn't count on her either. Turn.

Mason might come. Step, step. Turn.

There was a noise outside the tiny window, high up in the wall opposite the door. Despite herself, Callie was curious. She wanted to distract herself from her bleak thoughts and there seemed no better way to do that then by trying to get up to that window.

It was too high for her to comfortably see out without something to stand on. The narrow cot was bolted to the wall. Damn. She was going to have to work at this. Callie looked around the cell more closely. The two cots were the only real furniture in the room. There was straw on the floor, piled in the corners and at the edges. The floor beneath was rough stone bricks. Even if she knew how, Callie had no tools to try and dig out.

The walls were dirty gray stone. The blocks were large and roughly squared. There were little protuberances and jutting-out places where the bricks didn't fit together perfectly. The first time Callie looked, she hadn't noticed how many places the wall didn't fit well. Now she began to realize how she might be able to make it up to see out the window. There were some chains by the cots, but when Callie picked them up to see if she might use them she saw the thick staple that bolted them to the wall. She wouldn't be able to break it, not with her feeble strength. Even if she wasn't weak, she wouldn't be able to do anything against the rusty thick iron.

Just the idea of seeing the outside was enough for her. She had to do it. She had to know what was happening somewhere other than this little stone cell. She had to do something. Action meant not being idle. Action meant doing something. Action meant accomplishment. Callie couldn't stand the waiting. It was so hard to not know what to do. It gave her too much time to think. It gave her too much time to remember and regret.

After she looked at the wall for some minutes, she thought she saw a way up to the window. It would not be comfortable, especially since she was wearing cute little heels. They would not do well climbing walls. There wasn't anything else to do about it though, not if she wanted to see out. Besides, her shoes didn't matter anymore to her. It seemed a lifetime ago that she was so agonized over choosing the correct shoes to go with an outfit. How ridiculous.

Callie went back up to the wall. She would have to climb at least a foot and a half up off the ground to be able to see out. She would probably have to hold onto whatever was over the window to stay up there, too. She wouldn't be able to balance on the tiny ledges and also move her head around to look.

Briefly Callie wondered why she was trying to solve all the problems before she started. She reasoned that maybe it was so that she would be anticipating things that might make her job impossible. If she saw the problems beforehand, and ways around them, perhaps she was more assured of success. Or perhaps it was just a way to keep from remembering the other things she had been obsessing over. Either way, Callie was a little surprised at herself now. She didn't think she would have been this observant or motivated before.

She began to try to get up the wall. It took several false starts. She wasn't particularly experienced in rock climbing and the protuberances were quite small. However, she managed to finally get all the way up to reach into the window hole and grasp the grill that covered it. More effort and she was able to pull herself up enough to look out. The grill had very small openings in it. She couldn't really see out, but she could hear.

No one was out there now. Perhaps later she would be able to hear something worthwhile. Anyway, it was nice to know that she had enough power to get up there on her own. She jumped back down. Her climbing and landing after the jump were probably not good ones, but no one was here to give her style-points.

She sat back on her cot and examined herself to make sure she wasn't bleeding or anything else that might give her actions away. Several fingernails had broken, one quite short and was bleeding slightly. She sucked on that one for a moment.

Sienna was still sleeping, which was probably a good thing. There was a ringing cry from outside. It sounded a bit like a song. It went on for a few minutes and when it was over, there was a murmuring sound that Callie couldn't place. The sound went on for a few minutes also, and then it too died down.

It was some time after than call and the murmuring sound that there was a sound from outside the cell. Callie got up curiously and looked out the door as far as she could see with the bars impeding her. There seemed to be a few soldiers coming along very slowly. As Callie watched, one took something from another and handed it to someone in one of the cells. Then Callie understood: it was time to eat. This was the food.

Despite herself, Callie's stomach grumbled loudly. She got tired of that. It had been embarrassing back home. It was downright dangerous here. She didn't want to draw attention to herself; her stomach complaining audibly was not helping her at all. Everyone noticed her when it growled.

The soldiers were not moving quickly and Callie was able to watch them for a while before she thought they might see her. There were three of them: one would put something in a bowl, one would hand it through, and the last marked something off on a clipboard. There was not a lot of conversation between the three. They almost seemed bored by it all.

When they had come nearer, Callie drew back from the door. She didn't want to antagonize them by staring or obviously watching. Sienna had warned against eye-contact in the truck. Callie figured she probably meant in here too.

She sat, waiting and looking only at her knees. She heard the cart moving along slowly, the slop of the food, a few grunts or soft voices. Once, she heard someone laugh harshly. It was probably one of the soldiers, but Callie didn't know what they were laughing at. It didn't really matter, except that she was interested in knowing what they thought funny. Laughing was something that only people did, and it made her guards seem a little more human.

The cart made its slow way closer. Callie continued to keep her eyes down. The soldiers were obviously nearing the end of the chore. They were starting to talk to each other a bit more. Callie thought she heard something about what one of them hoped to do once he was off duty. The others laughed.

"You should find one yourself!" One of them said, obviously in response. They were much closer, maybe even right outside her cell. Callie dared not look.

Chapter 18

They were right outside. Callie could tell by the way that the cart squeaked to a stop and the rustle of the soldiers' uniforms. She continued to look at her feet.

"You could do with one of these." One of the soldiers said.

Another snorted. "These? Neither of them has enough to make half a real woman. Too scrawny."

"Ah well. There must be some interest."

"There is. Misguided fools."

"Come now, they are at least very pretty little toys that Emil has picked up."

"Pretty. Yes, they are that, but I still prefer a woman who will not snap in two."

"Sometimes the steel is hidden deep."

"Ah, that may be. Is that a proverb?"

"It should be, if it is not."

"So spake the soldier of Allah!"

One of the others laughed. "Well, let us get this done. It stinks in here."

There was a noise of food being put in bowls and then there was a tapping on the door bars. "Come on now, girl." One of the soldiers said.

Callie stood up, still looking fixedly down. It was awkward to take the bowls without looking but she managed it.

"At least these act properly."   One of the men noted.

"True."

Callie heard the cart start to creak away, then there was a loud snapping sound.

"What did you do?" One man demanded.

"I just pushed it. The handles have broken." Another said.

"It must be repaired. We have no other."

"We'll do it. We broke it." The third soldier said.

"You must."

"We are filled with remorse.   When must it be back?"

"We need it again by the midday call. We give water in the morning."

"We shall have it back. A thousand apologies!"

The other man sighed loudly. "It is an old cart. Make sure it is back."

"Of course, of course!"

The voices faded out. Callie sat on her cot and looked at the food. She had no idea if she should wake Sienna or not. Maybe she needed to sleep, but she also needed to eat. Callie sighed. This was all very confusing. It would be much easier if she knew what to do.

Sienna did not wake up for quite a while. Callie was almost tempted to leave her alone. Sienna hadn't eaten hardly anything recently though. Callie wasn't that unobservant. She'd seen that Sienna had eaten almost nothing before her wedding and very little after. She must eat something.

"Come on, Sienna. Wake up, please. You have to eat." Callie pleaded half to herself. She wasn't sure Sienna could hear her. Finally, Sienna sighed and rolled over.

"What was that?" She whispered.

"You need to eat." Callie repeated, placing the bowl on the floor and helping Sienna to sit up. "Please, just a little?"

"Oh, I suppose I can try." Sienna said without much conviction. Callie put the bowl on her lap and went back to her own cot. She managed to eat the food, whatever it was. The whole time, she carefully watched Sienna. Sienna took a few bites then she quit and stared off at the wall.

Callie wasn't sure how long they had before the soldiers came back for the bowls. No matter what she said, Sienna didn't seem to hear her, nor would she eat anymore. Callie was convinced that Sienna was becoming too isolated to be able to act. This could have some serious repercussions for them both.

Callie began to be seriously afraid that she might have to act on her own without any guidance whatsoever. She had known it before, but the reality had somehow stayed from her. Sienna was so capable, so sure of herself. Now, though, she was numb and frozen. Callie had to face the real possibility that Sienna wouldn't be able to do anything at all.

As they sat waiting for the soldiers to reappear, Callie shivered. She wasn't ready to have to deal with this type of thing, not at all. She had no training, and no idea of how she was supposed to act. She wanted to curl up and have everything have been a dream. Maybe even wake up and go to the jewelry store and see James there.

It didn't happen. Instead, after waiting for what seemed like a long time, Callie gave it up. She reasoned that even if the soldiers usually came back, maybe they wouldn't tonight since the cart had broken. She set her bowl down and looked around rather at a loss. What should she do now? She was going to have to do something.

The window high up beckoned invitingly again. It was a link to outside. It was proof that the world was not enclosed in this small cell and it extended beyond the reality she was in.

A quick glance at Sienna showed Callie that she had fallen asleep again. Callie gently took the bowl from where it was cradled in Sienna's lap and set it on the floor. Carefully, she directed Sienna to lie down again. It seemed a safer place to be to Callie. Sienna didn't wake up, and Callie quietly went back to the wall with the window to try and see or hear something.

It was dark outside. There were no people to be seen or heard, except a soft pacing of the night sentry. He passed close enough for Callie to hear his steps but not through her limited view. The air that wafted in was much cooler than it had been earlier. The desert lost its warmth rapidly. Callie welcomed the coolness. She was a little more at home with it. Feeling something other than hot dry air made her feel that she was still in control of something, even though it was precious little. The cool air made her feel a little like she was still connected with her life far away.

Even as she got back down, Callie realized that she would also have to sleep. The cool air was enough to sleep in. As she closed her eyes, Callie was struck by a ridiculous idea: she imagined some of the girls she had hung out with back home passing by her door right now. The looks on their faces were shocked and judging and Callie found she didn't care in the least. Somehow, she had changed. She wasn't interested in the opinions of those socialites anymore. She gave them all a mental middle finger and rolled over to face the wall. One of Porter's favorite swearing phrases came and she smiled.

"Fuck you all. You can all go to fucking Hell." She whispered and closed her eyes.

Chapter 19

Callie slept. She may have dreamed, but she didn't remember any of them. She woke a few times, once when Sienna was sobbing in her sleep, but nothing else seemed to be memorable from the night.

Towards morning, Callie awoke shivering. The air was decidedly chilly. Perhaps that was normal for the desert. It seemed like she had read or heard something about that once. Whether that was true or not, Callie was cold now. There was no blanket, of course, and it seemed like it wasn't dawn yet. That probably meant that it would not get warmer for a long while, several hours at least. So much for sleep, Callie thought. Oh well. She would sleep later on in the day, when it was too hot again to do much else. Right now, she was going to have to move around to warm up. Her teeth were actually chattering.

"How the hell does anyone even live here?" She muttered to herself. She stood up, waving her arms energetically in circles. This was ridiculous. She also tried jumping up and down. Eventually, it began to make her warmer. That blood circulating was making a huge difference. It also was waking her up. Callie knew she'd get cold again if she tried sleeping, so that was out as an option. She was pretty tired still, but it would have to wait. A glance over at Sienna made her fairly sure that she was still asleep, and she didn't seem as cold as Callie. Maybe her body was better for this area. Who knew? Callie shrugged. Let her sleep.

Callie climbed the wall again, but it was a bit harder today. She was sore from everything yesterday, and the fingernail she'd torn was infected and hurt. Damn. Once up there, Callie saw that the sky was a light blue along what horizon she could see and dark higher up. The sun must be close to rising. She couldn't see any stars in the thin strip of sky in her view. Even if there had been some, Callie didn't know enough about the night sky to know which way she was facing. Too bad she'd never thought to study stuff like that before.

Callie would have stayed up longer, but her arms were starting to shake. She just wasn't strong enough to hold herself there long and her muscles were sore from yesterday. Silently, she cursed her lack of strength. She'd never been strong, and she felt it now. If she could just stay up there a little longer, maybe she would hear something worth hearing!

As it was, she dropped back to the floor inside. It probably wasn't even the fact that she could hear outside up there, Callie realized. It was the connection to outside, to somewhere free. Somewhere outside the walls of this cell. She felt so trapped and helpless inside. Seeing and hearing outside helped her feel like she wasn't stuck. It reminded her that there was more to this world than the walls of this little block room. It gave her reason to fight the numbness.

There was a floating singing call outside. It was followed by a murmuring, like the night before. Callie had no idea what it was. It wasn't even dawn yet. Who or what would that cry signify?

As the light began to creep into the room, it became colder. Callie had thought the sun would bring heat, but if it was, it wasn't doing it very quickly. Callie had to start doing physical movement again to try and stay warm. This seemed silly. It should get warmer not colder. She kept moving. The cute heels were too cumbersome. She kicked them off and jumped around on the cool floor. It wasn't too cold at least. Small victories, Callie, small victories, she thought. Any victories might have been closer.

The air grew warmer imperceptivity. It took what seemed like hours. Callie couldn't keep moving the whole time, but she stayed reasonably warm. She smiled slightly when she remembered how hot it had been yesterday. Undoubtedly, she would be complaining about the heat soon. It was probably a commentary on something. Like the fickleness of her. Oh well. She kept moving for the time being.

It was warm enough now that she didn't have to keep flapping around like a flightless bird. There was a creaking sound outside the cell. Callie went to the door and looked out. Two soldiers, different than last night's, were doling out something that looked like water. The bowls were handed out from the other rooms, so Callie quickly found hers. Sienna hadn't eaten much, so Callie dumped it out and kicked straw over it. There didn't seem to be any dairy in it. It probably wouldn't stink. It seemed pretty dry in the bowl. Most likely, it would just dry into cement-hard blobs. That was what Callie hoped, at least.

Sienna stirred. Callie put the bowls down and went to her friend. Sienna sighed and opened her eyes. She didn't seem as distant as yesterday.

"They're bringing us water. Are you all right?" Callie whispered.

Sienna sighed again. "Not really, but I think I am a little better."

"Good. I was really worried about you yesterday."

"It's not over yet, Callie."

Callie nodded even though she wasn't sure what Sienna was referring to. It might have been herself, and it might have been the situation. Maybe it was both.

Callie watched carefully. Sienna seemed a lot less wooden. That was encouraging. If she could function, they had more of a chance.

"Sienna, what should I do?"

Sienna thought about it silently, staring blankly at the wall. Finally, she said, "I'm not totally sure. What has happened?"

"Not much, really. At least, not here. I can get up to that window, but that is all I have managed."

"Good for you, Callie. Who knows? That might be very helpful. I suppose we haven't been in this shitty place long?"

"A day, really. This is the morning. They are bringing water right now. I don't make any eye contact still."

"Wise woman that you are."

Callie smiled.

The sounds of the soldiers outside with the water were closer. Sienna glanced at Callie in warning and Callie nodded. They were quiet as the soldiers approached. They both kept their faces down as they accepted their water in the bowls.

Once the soldiers had gone, Callie drank all her water at once. It was warm but she didn't mind. The dry air of this desert baked the moisture out of her.

"How do people even live here?" She demanded in a despairing tone.

Sienna smiled. "Come now, you know people survive where they have to."

"True." Callie sighed. "I guess we should probably sleep then."

"Probably, unless you have something more interesting to do. It is too fucking hot for much."

"More interesting? Gee, I think I forgot to bring my card deck, so I guess sleep it is." Callie said, pretending to look through the pockets of her skirt. As she smiled at Sienna, she felt something in her pocket. The soldiers hadn't checked their clothes, and she felt a chain from a broken gold necklace in there. The clasp had snapped and she put in her pocket to not lose it. Unfortunately, that was the only thing she had in her pockets. Too bad. For a second she'd hoped to find something more useful.

Sienna laughed, shaking her head at Callie. "That was a major oversight, my dear!"

"I know. I shall have to do better next time." Callie agreed, sitting back on her own cot. She was a little surprised at herself. She didn't usually make jokes like this. She had always been too shy around Sienna. Maybe James and Porter were wearing off on her. They were always kidding each other.

Callie began to feel tired again. Getting up so early was not her usual method and she began to feel sluggish and slow. She was grateful that Sienna was awake and talking though. She seemed to have worked through her personal tragedy at least a little.

Even as she thought about how glad she was to have someone to talk to, Callie realized that she didn't really know Sienna very well. She'd always been too intimidated. Sienna was gorgeous, and she always seemed so in charge of situations. Callie had been shy because she'd felt overshadowed. The first time Callie had met her was when James had brought her to the store to show her around. They'd only just started dating, and Callie was terribly shaken to find Sienna working there. Even knowing of Sienna's involvement with Porter didn't seem to lessen her insecurity.

She had been certain that James couldn't be as interested in her as he must be in Sienna. He must just be using her as a second-best replacement. She was jealous and felt sure that James would default to Sienna if he could.

He never had, and she had come to be at least comfortable around Porter and Sienna, but she always felt shy and overshadowed anyway. At least she had finally conquered the raging jealousy. Sienna had told her rather bluntly that James had no interest in her romantically and he was completely faithful to Callie. Callie still kind of worried, sometimes.

Now, as she tried to fall asleep, Callie felt a different kind of overshadowing. She knew Sienna didn't mean to make her feel inadequate; she'd just done so much and been so many places. How could Callie measure up to that? At least this time, it was a relief to let Sienna take charge. She didn't like the idea that a mistake of hers could send both of them to death. It was frightening, and Callie had agonized over decisions. Sienna was awake and she could take charge.

Callie even felt a little secure as she drifted into sleep. She didn't have to worry over her decisions anymore. It was a great weight off her.

Chapter 20

Over the course of the morning, Callie drifted in and out of sleep a few times. It was getting hot, and the last time she woke up sweating. Damn desert, anyway! She shifted around a few times, but sleep was elusive. Oh well. She would still lay here and just sort of drowse. It wasn't like she had any appointments to keep. Not until lunchtime, at least.

She hadn't quite realized how much freer she felt now that she knew Sienna was in charge. The experience the woman had was immense, especially when it came to fighting. Callie had nothing to go on for actual physically fighting. Her social standing had meant that she was considered too lady-like to indulge in such things, especially since she wasn't as eccentric as some of her friends had been. She didn't want to stand out, and that meant not doing things different from other girls.

Once they got home, she should start taking lessons. If anyone said anything about it, she would give them the middle finger. Then Callie realized she was planning things after they got home. She had already started to get ready for it. It might take a long time, but with Sienna's help, she was sure they would get there someday. It seemed a little absurd to Callie, but she was planning all the same. It no longer seemed like a possibility; it seemed like a certainty.

It must have been close to lunch time when she was distracted from her drowsing state by footsteps outside. They caught her attention because they were so different. The soldiers who had come before had walked with a certain purposefulness. These footsteps were hesitating and quiet. Callie thought they sounded a little guilty, somehow.

She realized there were whispers, too. Low voices muttered to each other. Callie, always curious, tried to hear what they were saying but it was frustratingly just beyond her hearing. She couldn't quite make distinct words.

It seemed that the voices came to a stop right outside the door of their cell. At least they had to be close when the footsteps ceased. Callie knew she couldn't risk looking outside to see what was happening; it was far too dangerous to try. Sienna had confirmed that already. The situation began to feel tense. She was edgy about all this. It seemed very strange, but then again, this whole situation was strange to her.

Callie mentally shrugged and put her head down again, trying to shake off that tense feeling. She'd stay alert, of course, but chances were that it was nothing to worry about. She would share it with Sienna later. It couldn't hurt to be prepared if something came from it.

Gradually, Callie became aware of a stealthy scratching noise at the cell door. She was struck again by the hesitating quality of it. It was as if someone was trying to be inconspicuous in an unknown environment and overplaying the part. The tense feeling began to grow and Callie realized she had been wrong: this was not something that would happen later. It was happening now and she was scared.

The lock clicked. Someone outside said something, low and hoarse. The click might have been too loud, or perhaps it had taken too long. Callie wasn't sure and there was no way for her to know. The only thing she felt reasonably certain of was the tone of reprimand.

Softly, the door swung open. The hinges weren't very good, probably from a combination of dryness, dust, and general neglect. They squeaked in protest. The sound was shocking only because the room was so quiet.

Callie had no chance wake Sienna to ask for guidance. It had happened too quickly. The three men were already in the room. Almost ironically, the small size of the room was the one saving grace: the door wouldn't close and it was still ajar. It might have been an oversight. There was no way to know. Callie saw that it was still opened slightly and then the men were all she could see.

The men were dressed in the usual soldiers' uniforms as far as Callie could tell. They looked indiscernible from the dozens of other soldiers she'd seen so far. She forgot that she wasn't supposed to look up, she was surprised. She stared at them, trying to figure out what they were there for.

This seemed a little strange to Callie. She was confused by this new development. Were they here to take Sienna and herself somewhere? Did Emil have some other plan for them?

One of the men looked at Callie and she became instantly afraid. He looked both desperately hungry and desperately angry. This was not right, not right at all. She instinctively tried to back away but was hindered by the wall. She was up against it and could go no farther. There was no escape.

"Emil is a fool. I will take what I want. He can forbid as he sees fit and shout at Allah for it all. He is no man. He does not burn with right desires." The soldier staring at Callie said to the others. "I shall teach this one who owns the desert."

The other two smiled and nodded. One reached out and grasped Sienna's shoulder. She came awake instantly. The difference was that she didn't try to run. She came up fighting.

She kicked and punched, trying anything she could. It wasn't much good against two large men.

One of them took a blow to the face and his head jerked back but the other was already there and caught her arm roughly.

That was all Callie saw. The man in front of her, his face contorted with rage, reached her and had her arm in a very hard grip. He tried to pull her skirt up with his other hand.

Callie screamed, panicking, and tried to kick and push him away. She was only reacting. She didn't know what to do. Every detail became crisp and sharp and incredibly detailed to Callie as she kept struggling, screaming the whole time.

The man's face became even more angry and frightening. It was like he was consumed by hate. He hit Callie in the face very hard. Then his hand closed around her throat and he lifted her and slammed her back against the wall.

Callie grasped at his arm, trying to give herself enough room to breathe. He was choking her with one hand. Uselessly, she scratched at his hand and arm. Her feet scrabbled at the wall. One of them found a tiny ledge and she pushed against it to try and release some of the

129

pressure her body weight was putting on her throat. The rough stone dug into her shoulder blades and back.

The soldier ripped her blouse open with his free hand. Callie heard the cotton tear and buttons hit the wall and floor. She was so terrified that all her thoughts were consumed with the one idea of getting away. She had to get away! She kept her desperate struggles up even as she started to lose consciousness from lack of oxygen.

As the room started to get fuzzy in her vision, Callie saw some other men rush in. The door hadn't been closed, she remembered, and these new soldiers slammed it all the way open. The soldier who had her against the wall jerked his head towards the interruption.

One of the new soldiers was a big man, bigger by far than anyone else in the room; he came straight at the soldier holding Callie by her throat. In alarm, the man loosed his grip and she slid down the wall. This new turn of events did not reassure her. She still was terrified and cowered on her cot, too afraid to move. The big man hit the other soldier and sent him to the back of the cell with the punch. He crumpled there. The other two were thrown back as well by the other two soldiers.

The big soldier stood over the three vanquished. He looked at one of the other two new soldiers. "Someone better go and get Emil. This is serious."

One of the other two nodded. "You are right." He nudged the third. "Go. Get him. He must come himself."

"I understand. I will persuade him." The third left.

Callie was still unsure of what was happening. She couldn't quite believe that these new soldiers weren't out to do the same thing. The big man glanced at her quickly. "These girls are terrified. Can we move them somewhere safer?"

The other shook his head. "Not without Emil or one of the generals."

The big one shrugged. He kept close eye on the three sitting in sullen silence at the back of the cell. Callie tried to pull her blouse closed, but all the buttons had been torn off. She had to hold it closed. She was still afraid. It seemed like she might be safer now, though. These new men didn't seem interested in what the first group had been.

There were hurried footsteps outside. The third soldier must have been amazingly eloquent because he returned quickly with Emil and several other men. Emil stared at the three at the back who looked suddenly very afraid.

His lip curled into a sneer. "These are not worthy of my army. Take them and dispose of them, immediately. I do not want them to have a chance to poison any of the others."

One of the men who had come with him saluted sharply. The big man had to back out of the cell and then they removed the three men, all of whom were saying things in a confused mess of babbling. Callie shuddered to hear them crying and begging. She was seized with violent trembling.

Emil came into the cell and dispassionately examined Callie's face, arm, and throat. She shook the whole time, so afraid and tired that she could hardly focus.

Sienna fared worse; the shock of the attempted rape on top of everything she had experienced was too much finally. When Emil took her arm, Sienna went crazy. That was all Callie could call it. She was screaming and kicking and fighting. Emil stepped back hurridly. He motioned the big soldier back in. "Make sure she doesn't hurt herself until Usama can get the drug into her."

"Which drug, Emil?" Someone asked respectfully.

"The one that will make her quiet, idiot." Emil snapped, turning away from Sienna dismissively. "She has to be calm on the block tomorrow. This other too. Drug them both." He left the room.

Callie was still shaking. Her mind was slowly processing what was happening. She thought she knew what the next thing would be. It had to be some sort of drug that would make Sienna and herself into lethargic and safe bodies. Once she thought it through, Callie realized she had to get out of taking the drug. She would have to convince whoever brought it that she didn't need it. Whatever she had to say or do, she had to convince that man. She had to stay conscious and competent.

She had to lie or cheat to get out of that drug. Sienna couldn't be the leader anymore, and there wasn't a good way to get her out of taking it. She may have been a consummate actress, but the stress was too much for her this time. Callie had to do it. She hated it, but she had to. No one else was going to be coming to save them now.

Usama came back with a small bottle and two syringes. Sienna was still fighting the big man's restraints and sobbing. Callie was at first afraid that she would get more hurt by the soldier who was holding her but he seemed to be very gentle if only slightly more movable than a mountain. Nothing Sienna tried made any difference in his restraint.

Usama gestured the other soldier forward, the one who had fetched Emil. He came and assisted Usama by holding Sienna's arm still while the syringe was filled and then injected.

Sienna arched and screamed, but gradually she fell silent and limp, her eyes dull.

"And this other one, now." Usama grunted.

"Wait, please!" Callie said desperately. She got on her knees on the floor, begging and looking at Usama pleadingly. "I have to stay awake. I have to help her. Please! I promise to be good! I have had some bad reactions to drugs before. I don't want to die. I have to protect my friend. Please!" Usama hesitated, looking at the big soldier and the other uncertainly. Callie pressed on. "I can give you the only payment I have. Look! It's gold! I only have this left! Please!" She held out the broken chain in supplication, looking down finally. She felt like he was going to take it and she didn't want to offend him by looking at him too long.

Usama wavered. Finally, he took the chain. He looked significantly at the other soldiers. "This never happened. I have given them both the drugs, as ordered. If you say anything different..."

"No sir, never!" They assured him quickly.

Usama nodded. He pocketed the bottle and chain and left the cell.

The big soldier looked at the other. "We have to get the food out to the prisoners. These two should be okay."

The second soldier nodded. "Will you be able to keep this one alive?" He asked Callie, gesturing towards Sienna. Callie was staring at his ankles so as to not give offense again.

Callie nodded, still on her knees on the floor. "Yes, sir. Thank you, sir."

"If you think she is not doing well, let us know and we will get the antidote."

"Yes, sir." Callie said again. They left and closed the cell door firmly behind them. Callie was suddenly seized by the violent urge to throw up. She fought it, but she knew she was losing. Weakly, she tottered to the back of the cell to the hole that served as a privy and vomited everything up. It was all just too fucking hard!

Chapter 21

Self-pity is never an attractive thing. Callie was very glad that no one could see her as she sat in her private misery, huddled on her cot and shaking violently. She started to cry again. It was all so unfair. She couldn't lead anybody, she had no experiences, and yet she was the one in charge. This was definitely not what she wanted. How the hell was she supposed to pull anything good out of this shit?

Sienna was completely out of the mix now. Callie had to check on her and make sure she didn't die. And she had to think of a way to keep them both from getting into more trouble before the sale. And she had to keep her own shit together for after the sale. And she had to try and think of some way to escape. And she had to try and meet any other challenges that might show up.

This was too much for her. She wasn't nearly the leader that other people were. She wasn't even capable of fighting her way out of a situation; the encounter with the three soldiers had shown that rather convincingly. She had been man-handled with so much ease she felt almost like she hadn't done anything right at all. Sienna was so much better; why hadn't she been the one to be in charge? Callie even felt a surge of resentment towards Sienna. She was out now and Callie was going to have to deal with her, too! Fucking wasn't fair at all!

Sienna's dull gaze didn't change as Callie glared at her. Her head was loose and lay to the side, her arms limp. Callie drew herself up mentally as she looked at Sienna. What the hell was she doing, anyway? Like Sienna had tried to get herself drugged into insensibility. Sienna hadn't meant to have three soldiers try to rape them. Why the hell was she blaming this on Sienna? And, for that matter, why was she angry at her?

Callie couldn't blame her own fucking shortcomings on someone else. It wasn't something she should be doing to a friend. She dared to think that Sienna was her friend. Friends shouldn't dump shit on friends. Especially not since Sienna had helped so far. Callie had to be a grown up on her own.

134

Sighing slightly, she sniffed and wiped at her nose. "Dammit, Callie, pull it together." She muttered to herself, sitting up straighter. As if she had the water in her to put on an extended weeping session. How ridiculous she was. She was sure to dehydrate quickly herself this way.

The soldiers were right outside her cell. She hadn't noticed them there she was so involved in her private pity-party. Now, one of them tapped the bars impatiently.

"Come on, girl. We need the bowls."

"Oh!" She stood up, still very unsteady and immediately had to sit down again. Throwing up had robbed her of most of the strength she'd had left. Crying had not made her feel better, either.

"You know, they are awfully weak still." The big soldier said to the one in charge. Callie recognized his voice. "Maybe, just this time, could we take their food in to them?"

There was a long pause, then the one in charge sighed loudly. "All right, but this didn't happen."

"Understood. Would you unlock the door for us? We'll do it." There was the click of the lock and the door squeaked open.

Callie slumped back on the cot. It had been so much effort to stand up. She was intensely grateful to the soldiers. "Thank you, sirs." She whispered weakly, staring at the floor fixedly.

"It is nothing." The other said, placing the bowl beside her. There was a short silence as they gave Sienna her food. "Uh, sir? This one is not doing well under influence of that drug. Maybe we should give her an antidote or something?" The other said to the one still outside. He sounded concerned.

"What? I must check." The one in charge pushed his way to Sienna, and Callie couldn't see what happened. He stood up a few seconds later. "You are right. We'll have to give her the stuff. I have it here. It should help. Hold her arm for me."

Again, Callie couldn't see anything because the soldier blocked her view. Then he stood up and left the cell. "Make sure of that other one." He called over his shoulder. "I will make the proper marks on the

135

tally." The second soldier grunted and also left the cell.

The big one turned to Callie. "Are you all right?" He asked perfunctorily.

Callie nodded. She felt a growing suspicion. That voice, and the way he moved on his feet, lightly, balanced. Something about it triggered her memory. She thought she recognized it. If she had been less tired or less stressed, she would have been less rash. As it was, the surge of realization made her look up at the soldier full in the face.

"Michael?" She whispered.

"Shh, don't let on that you know." He breathed back as he leaned over and pretended to do something close to her. His face was deadly serious behind the dark skin and black hair and beard.

Callie nodded dumbly. This was too much to hope for and yet she was seeing him. It was really Michael. There was no doubt now. She was a little surprised that she had recognized him solely from his way of moving, though. She would never have thought she had been observant enough to know him from any number of other men. And yet, she had known him. It had taken a long time it was true, but she had done it. She had. Callie. Not Sienna, although she might have if she hadn't been so far introverted. Callie almost started crying again, with relief.

"Just fucking stay calm." Michael continued in that same soft whisper. "You'll be okay."

"Are you going to take us now?" Callie whispered.

"We can't, Callie. Not right now. There's no damn way."

"Oh. I just…"

"I know. It has to be later."

The soldier outside stuck his head back in. "Are you finished yet?"

"Yes, sir. This one should be okay, but we'll need to check on her again this evening." Michael responded louder to the officer.

"Of course. I shall inform Usama about the antidote. I think she will remain as she is now, but she should be able to walk for the sale."

Michael nodded and left as if he had no interest in the cell at all. The door shut and Callie felt a tiny resentment within her. They could have taken her out now. Then she sighed. Of course they couldn't. Michael would never leave a woman in such a horrible place, especially not after what had happened earlier. It must be impossible to take Sienna and her. She was going to have to resign herself to it.

All the same it was hard to stay behind as that door shut again. She was so close to freedom, and it had been cut off again. Callie was actually a little surprised at how much she had yearned to be free, once she knew it was Michael. The realization brought an instant, irrational thought that they would be taking them out immediately. It made no sense. She just thought, somehow, they'd pulled such miraculous things before; they'd be able to do it again.

Anticipation was much harder to live through, she decided. Instead of just concentrating on acting correctly, now she was going to have to act like she was the same as before she knew it was Michael. In hindsight, that was probably why he hadn't let her know initially.

Callie wished she hadn't found him out. But then she was glad she had. She was dreadfully confused by both feelings: it shouldn't have made this much difference, should it? Maybe it should. It didn't really matter; it was done now and she had to deal with it. Giving herself a stern mental shake, she picked up the bowl from beside her and ate the tasteless stuff. It actually helped. Any food seemed to be comforting right now.

Callie sighed and leaned her head back on the wall. She closed her eyes and stopped thinking about anything. Just being quiet and sitting was all she wanted to do for now. The air was warm and she breathed in slowly, sinking into the very act of breathing. It was all she wanted to do. She listened to herself breathe, felt herself breathe, and that was all. She didn't fall asleep. That would have brought on dreams. Dreams had a way of being more frightening than refreshing sometimes. She merely sat and calmed herself and became empty for a while.

Things happened outside the cell; there was that haunting cry, murmuring, shuffling, sighing, voices in and out. This was not a quiet place during the day. Callie allowed the sounds to wash over her without paying any of them particular note. She kept her eyes closed and didn't concentrate on anything. She might have even drifted off to sleep, although she wasn't sure. She just settled into herself. It was one of the most delicious things she'd ever done.

Chapter 22

Some time later, Callie wasn't sure how long later, of course, she came back to herself. Strangely, she felt more calm and determined than she had before. Maybe there was something to that whole contemplation or meditation or whatever it was that church said that Porter talked about with James sometimes.

Whatever it was that made her feel better, she was grateful. Now to see about Sienna. The soldiers had given her something else. Callie wasn't very well-versed in her drugs, but she suspected that even if she had been it wouldn't make any difference. She couldn't do anything beyond what she already had.

The coincidence that she had the one thing in her pocket that had made the soldier motivated to not give her the drugs wasn't lost on her. Many items might have been more useful immediately but it was doubtful now if any would have worked for the end goal. Gold spoke a language that was universal. She had been very lucky to have that broken necklace after all. She still would welcome something more useful, like a knife, but hey, she was doing all right with what she had.

Sienna was still far from lucid. Callie checked her pulse and breathing. Sienna still had the same glassy expression, her face wooden.

"Sienna? Can you hear me?" Callie asked softly.

Sienna's eyes swung slowly and dully around to look at Callie. She didn't say anything. Any movement was a good thing, in Callie's opinion.

"Sienna, my dear, can you eat anything?"

Again, Sienna seemed to take a long time to process what Callie had said. Finally, with what seemed to be a supreme effort, she whispered, "Yes."

"I am going to give you some food. You don't have to chew it, just swallow. I'll do it very slowly, so that you don't choke or anything, okay?"

After an agonizingly long time, Sienna again said, "Yes."

Callie was encouraged by the interaction. She carefully helped prop Sienna's head up and gently gave her a few tiny morsels of the tasteless stuff. "I think maybe that is enough for now. Maybe we can try some more later?"

Sienna closed her eyes without responding. Callie laid her back down as gently as she could and tried to make her comfortable. It was probably true that Sienna couldn't feel much in this drugged sleep. Callie still didn't want her to have sore spots when she woke up if it could be avoided. She may not know what was coming in the next few days, but she could do what she would want someone to do for her.

The earlier excitement suddenly took its toll. Callie began to shake and felt drained. She sighed and lay on her own cot. God, but she hated feeling incompetent. With only the slightest whimper, Callie gave it all up and fell asleep. It was just too much and she couldn't keep it up for any longer.

Hopefully, it would get better.

Callie didn't sleep very long. At least it didn't seem very long to her. Since the only way she had to judge time was Michael and the food cart, she hadn't any real idea how long she had slept. Michael wasn't outside anywhere, so therefore, she only knew it was afternoon sometime.

"Fucking inconsiderate to take my goddamn watch." Callie muttered. She had not woken up in a good mood. She sighed and stretched. Her neck had a terrible crick in it and it was painful to turn her head to the left or raise her arm too high. This had fun written all over it.

Sienna was awake, but she still couldn't sit up or do much. Callie figured she should probably try and give her some more food, even though she was herself in a terribly rotten mood. It didn't matter how she felt; she had to help Sienna. Callie wasn't even sure Sienna would do it for her. She only knew that if she could, she had to try. If she could do something but ignored her friend, she knew she would feel guilty for a long time. It was just the way it was.

"Okay, Sienna. Let's try to eat some more. I am warning you that I am in a fucking awful mood though, so I apologize in advance for anything I do or say that is way harsh."

Sienna gave the faintest smile and her eyes sparkled. Callie felt resentful. Since when was she worth laughing at? She was trying her hardest!

"Thank you." Sienna whispered softly. It was barely audible.

"Oh, you're welcome. I am truly sorry that I am pissy. Here, here's your food." As she gave the tiniest little pieces to Sienna, Callie tried to focus on what she was doing, not on how she felt. The resentful feeling was fading a little, or maybe she just didn't have any attention to spare for it. Whichever it was, by the time Sienna was finished with the food, a chore that probably took at least half an hour, Callie felt better. Her neck still ached abominably but she felt more at ease.

Sienna closed her eyes and lay back again. Without opening her eyes, she whispered slowly, "Feel better?"

Callie laughed in spite of herself. "Yes, I suppose I do. I shouldn't feel so upset with you. That makes no sense at all."

Sienna smiled slightly again, her eyes still closed. "Makes sense to me. I'm fucking annoying."

Callie was shocked by that. "No, Sienna! No! It's my problem."

"Callie, please, I can't even fucking sit up. I'm annoying. I'd be more worried if you weren't pissed."

Callie didn't know how to respond to that. It wasn't true, now that she thought about it. The truth was probably that both of them were right and wrong. Actually, that was probably true of almost everything in the world, with the notable exception that this situation was fucked up. No one would disagree with that.

"Okay, Sienna, you're right and I am right. Both of us. We're in it together, we might as well both be right."

Sienna opened her eyes and smiled a bigger smile than she had yet at Callie. "Oh, my dear, you are a treasure. Thank God you are here!"

Callie smiled back shyly. "Oh, Sienna, I am still so scared." She confessed in a low voice.

"So am I. But right now, I must sleep some more. I don't know what tomorrow holds, and I might need strength."

"Of course." Callie helped her get comfortable and retreated

141

back to her own cot. She considered the situation a bit more. Although she was tired, she knew that if she took more naps, she wouldn't be able to sleep at night, and she really wanted to sleep at night. Callie was still a little afraid of the dark. She always had the vague feeling that something was going to sneak up behind her and she wouldn't see it. It didn't make much logical sense, especially not in this cell.

There was the singing cry outside followed by the soft murmuring. Once it was finished, the door at the end of the corridor opened. Callie looked out her own door. It was Michael and the others with the dinner. She would have to be patient and see what they would do.

Before they were halfway down the hallway, though, the door opened again. It was Emil and several other men in uniforms. One of them held a tablet and appeared to be taking a tally. They brushed past the food cart without so much as a glance at the soldiers who were there. Emil was speaking to the group he had around him. Callie quickly lay on the cot and closed her eyes to pretend being asleep while listening as hard as she could.

"These will be sold the same way as usual." She heard Emil say crisply to the soldiers around him. "You all know what to do. However, we have several special ones this time. I want them on the block first. That way, bidders will not withhold their funds anticipating. And these," They had stopped outside the cell where Callie and Sienna were. "These must be first of all. They'll go up together. I want all the buyers to know about what we have sold, so when they go back to their cities, they will carry the name of Army of the Almighty with them."

"Yes, sir!" The one with the tablet said. "Do you want them specially clothed?"

Emil paused, thinking. "No, I do not think so. I want it clear that they are not from here, and I want it clear that they have been forcibly seized."

"Sir! They will be ready at first light tomorrow! Shackles?"

"Absolutely. We must convey the stature they occupy now."

There were murmurs of assent and the group moved back to the door discussing other statistics.

So it was on for tomorrow morning. Callie and Sienna would either be freed by Mason by then, or they would be soon after. Callie didn't know which although she wanted out as soon as it was possible. It wasn't helping her be patient knowing they would be rescued. That was probably one of the reasons they hadn't told her sooner.

Callie wasn't in the mood to be reasonable. She was still in a foul mood, and knowing that Michael was right out there and yet not going to do anything made her angry. She wanted to slam her fists against the wall or howl or scream or something. She wanted to do something violent so they would have to take her out now.

The food cart rolled wearily closer. Finally, it was outside the cell. Michael handed her the bowl, and while the other soldier chatted with the lead soldier, he breathed, "Don't do anything to draw attention. Just do what they tell you to."

"Fuck. You. I want fucking out." She hissed back.

"That's exactly what I am warning you against."

There wasn't time to say anything else. The lead soldier made his tally and they moved off, talking about the sale and how famous Emil was going to be. Like the soldiers in the truck, Callie seemed to note a decided lack of enthusiasm for the idea among the common soldiers.

"Yeah, I'll do what they fucking tell me. Fuck you, Michael. Fuck you too, Mason. I am so pissed with you two right now..." She couldn't think of something harsh enough to promise to do to them, so she let it trail off. Deep down, she knew she was being stupid about this, but it still hurt to be left behind. She hated having to wait for something to happen. She never had been patient enough for her teachers in finishing school. She fidgeted far too much for them, and she hadn't been able to force herself into patience after, either. Maybe someday she would magically find that waiting didn't bother her. But of course, she would have to wait for that. The irony was not lost on Callie, even in her black mood, and she smiled ruefully to herself.

She was being ridiculous again, but it didn't matter. No one was counting on her right now. No one would be hurt by her silliness, so why not give into it for a little while? The world was too goddamn serious anyway.

Chapter 23

Callie awoke rudely to harsh voices and clunks and clanging outside the cell door. It took a few moments for her to readjust to reality. She had never been one to wake gracefully, it was true. She blinked blurrily and tried to get her thinking organized even as the noises continued outside.

After she finally had everything in order, she stood and went to the door. Cautiously, she looked out. It would not do to be caught looking directly at someone on accident. Fortunately, there was enough bustle and people milling around that it didn't much matter. The activity was concentrated at the farther end of the hall, outside the room with the other women in it. Callie remembered them looking out from the black clothes, only their eyes visible.

Oh, that was right, the sale was today. She remembered Emil saying something about clothes, but she and Sienna weren't going to wear anything different. Except, he had said something about shackles. Callie shivered slightly. It wasn't warm yet and the thought of wearing chains scared her. It was such a strong physical message that she was a slave.

Michael had warned her to do what they told her. Submission was probably the only way she would be able to rebel. How bizarre that thought was, but it was true all the same. Only by working below the surface would Mason be able to sneak them out. If it were as easy as bursting the locks and pulling them out, they would have been gone long ago. And, undoubtedly, dead a long time ago. It seemed ages since Mahmoud's office when this had started. Callie was surprised to realize that it had only been a few days. The endless hours of being locked with only her thoughts made everything seem much longer. No wonder people went crazy in solitary confinement.

Callie gently shook Sienna awake. "Sienna, you'd better be awake. The sale is today, and I can't carry you."

Sienna sighed. "No, that's fine. I can walk." Callie thought she seemed a little numb, but there was nothing to do about it. She couldn't walk Sienna through anything because there was a knocking on the door to their cell just then.

"Are you up?" Someone asked loudly.

"Yes, yes sir!" Callie said in what she fervently hoped was a submissive voice. She really wasn't good at this.

"Good. The shackles will be here in five minutes, then you are going first."

Callie didn't say anything, and the guard moved off before she could think of how to respond.

"I hope we are together." She said to Sienna.

Sienna merely nodded. Callie was worried about this turn of events so she kept talking to her, making little observations and trying to engage her attention. Sienna responded with nods or other small movements, but she didn't say hardly anything.

The door to the cell opened with the usual squeals. It wasn't Michael who stood in the doorway, and Callie felt a little let down by that. She had still hoped that they would be rescued. But no. It looked like she and Sienna would have to go on the blocks after all. That idea made her more afraid than she thought it would. However, she had to push past all that. She had to do the right things now. It mattered more than it had before.

The soldier in the doorway gestured to someone outside. Callie kept looking down, even has her heart was racing and she trembled slightly.

Someone came in with clanking and jingling chains. He snapped them onto her wrists and ankles, locking the shackles closed with a big padlock. He turned to Sienna and put them on her, too. Then he turned back.

"Why are you shaking, girl?" He asked gruffly.

Callie knew it would be foolish to tell the truth, and it would be equally foolish to ignore the question. "Um, I am thirsty, sir. I haven't had any water this morning." There might have been some truth to that, she thought.

"Of course." The soldier turned and shouted out into the corridor, "Water in here. These two are first."

Callie kept her face down. There was some scuffling outside. The soldier who had put the chains on pulled her head up somewhat roughly. "Open your mouth." He said perfunctorily.

Callie hastened to obey. He poured water into her mouth and she swallowed. It had a sweet taste to it, as if there was something more than water in the bag. He gave her two more swallows and then gave some to Sienna.

Another soldier stood in the doorway. "Are these two ready yet?"

"Yes, sir." The soldier said, pulling Callie and Sienna up and pushing them gently towards the door. Callie found herself hampered by the leg shackles more than she'd thought she would be. How did people walk in these things, anyway?

"Come on, come on, girls." The soldier looked them over quickly. "Scrawny little chickens. Why would any want these?"" He smirked to the other two soldiers who were waiting with him.

One of them shrugged. The other smirked back. "I bet they have some uses."

"They must. I heard they are opening for two million."

"You are joking."

"No, I heard it from Usama himself." The soldier guided Callie by her upper arm towards the door. "Come on, girls. Let us not keep Emil waiting." They started down a long dark hallway.

Sienna still seemed wooden, and Callie glanced at her from time to time to make sure she was moving. Finally, they were told to stand still and wait and the soldiers went to do something somewhere else. Callie decided she needed to know what Sienna was thinking.

"Sienna," She whispered as softly as she could, "can you hear me?"

Sienna was still staring at the ground in front of them. She whispered back, "Yes."

"Are you going to be okay?"

Sienna still stared ahead. "I don't know. I can't focus."

"Okay. Well, I will be with you. Don't look up."

Sienna didn't say anything, and Callie hoped she'd heard. The door opened again and a soldier gestured sharply at them. "Get in here, and hurry."

Hurrying was, of course, out of the question. Even if Sienna had been capable of it, they were still trying to figure out the chains. As it was, they got through the door all right, but then there were stairs. Callie hadn't even considered that there might be stairs. Sienna almost fell on the first step and Callie took her weight on her shoulders. As she struggled to hold Sienna up without her hands, the soldiers muttered angrily. None of them tried to help, though. They were probably afraid to touch them in front of anyone else.

There was a babble of voices around her, but Callie was focused on getting herself and Sienna up the stairs and on to whatever faced them next, so she didn't really hear them. At least, she didn't pay any mind to the noise or try to understand what it might mean. Sienna was more important to her right now. They had to get up these damn stairs!

Finally, they both stumbled up all seven of them. Callie wondered momentarily if there was some significance to there being seven. Probably not, and she would never know anyway.

Once they were up, Callie looked at Sienna. "Are you all right?" She whispered.

"Yes, I think so." Sienna whispered back.

Callie took a deep breath. Now for whatever was next. She risked a quick glance up to try and prepare herself for what might be coming. There wasn't much to see, as they were on a landing and there were soldiers making a gauntlet-type of corridor leading towards somewhere else. They would have to walk through that line of men to the stage or whatever they would be on. Callie took a deep breath.

"Ready, then, Sienna?"

Sienna sighed. Callie had to assume that meant that she was ready. Together, they began to make their slow way forward, towards the

148

opening at the end of the line. Again, Sienna stumbled heavily against Callie's shoulder. Callie held her up as best she could with her own shackled hands. Sienna seemed to be at the end of whatever strength she possessed. Callie knew she herself was exhausted by the emotional and physical strain she'd been through. She couldn't tell what Sienna had experienced. She thought it must be at least as hard as what Callie had gone through. Callie was no virgin, she hadn't ever been married, and she certainly hadn't been with one man nearly as long as Sienna had. The attempted rape, the violent kidnapping, and the attempted or real murder of Porter must be crushing her, finally. Sienna had done a great deal in her life, but Callie had the sneaky suspicion that all of it was too much for her now.

She'd have to be strong for them both, at least until Mason got them out.

Chapter 24

Callie and Sienna made it to the end of the line of men. The sound that had not registered in Callie's consciousness suddenly intruded itself with surprising volume. Callie again glanced up, shocked by the babble of many voices. They were on a stage or platform, standing at the back. The room beyond was dusty and bright, windows streaming with light from high up in the walls and showing rays of thick dust swirling. The effect was both hypnotizing to Callie and vaguely menacing. The room itself was not adorned, and it was absolutely packed with men. There had to be at least a hundred pushed close together, the large doors at the back closed tightly. And they were all looking at her and Sienna.

The noise swelled as a hundred voices began to talk at once. To the left of the stage area, Emil sat on a raised platform, not quite as high as the stage but certainly above floor level. There was a table in front of him with a large stack of paper. Bills of sale maybe, Callie thought. It didn't really matter. He was enthroned, figuratively and literally.

Emil stood and clapped his hands sharply several times. The voices eventually died down to a dull background murmur. Emil gestured Callie and Sienna forward as he said imperiously, "Our sale begins! For those of you who are new to us, we have a very special auction before the usual slave sale. These two, you will note, are not the usual fare." He paused significantly, allowing the murmur to swell and back off once more.

Clearly, Callie thought, he knew his audience and how to appeal to them. Charisma and careful personal relations went a long way to make a desirable leader, and Emil could speak to those he wanted to impress.

Again, Emil clapped his hands. "These two are Americans, infidels from that land across the sea. I know there are many, perhaps even in this room, who have an abiding interest in the, shall I say, differences between our women and those from elsewhere?"

From the murmuring and the smirks she saw, Callie figured that it was more than just a few of these men who were interested in something
150

like that. Some looked merely bored, waiting for this to be over so they could move on with what they wanted to bid on. Some looked crestfallen, knowing perhaps that they could not afford them and desiring them all the same. Most looked actively interested, leering at the two of them as if they were no more than jewelry or a car or something in a store. Emil paused for a few minutes, allowing the buyers ample time to look Callie and Sienna over. Callie felt so very exposed. She couldn't hold her ruined blouse shut, she couldn't hide behind someone, she could hardly stand up straight. She wished agonizingly that there would be a hole that opened right under her and she could just disappear from sight.

That didn't happen, of course. Nothing happened, and Callie was stuck standing beside Sienna, completely at odds with the room and terrified. Someone in the front and to her left moved and she inadvertently glanced over. Quickly, she caught herself and looked back down, but before she remembered to act submissive she caught a quick look at the man. It was like a jolt of electricity went through her. He was dark-skinned and bearded, but she would have sworn that it was Porter. Something about the eyes...

Her heart began to beat so hard and fast Callie was suddenly afraid that she would pass out. Thinking rapidly, she knew she couldn't let on that she knew. Taking several deep breaths, she let them hiss out slowly. Her heart slowed somewhat. Suddenly, Callie realized there was no way to tell Sienna what she knew. A sense of terrible guilt came over her. She knew that her friend's husband was alive and here and she couldn't tell her.

Emil raised his hands again. The voices died back gradually. "This is a unique sale, and I am sure you all realize that the bids will be quite high for this portion. If you do not have the reserves, do not worry, my friends! There will be others to bid on, even as these will be the first of their type. Do not worry at all! Allah has smiled upon us all, and by His favor, we will take more of these infidels and subject them to the might of Allah." He paused, bowing reverently. The men of the room also bowed. Callie thought it must be a sign of respect for the name of Allah. Emil straightened again, assuming a businesslike attitude. "I have an opening bid that is for both these girls of two million rial. My auction master shall take over." He stepped aside and seated himself again behind the table. Another man stepped forward to take bids.

Callie couldn't really follow what happened. Some voices shouted things, others clapped or cheered, some yelled other things, the auctioneer said things, gesturing first towards them, then towards men in the audience. It was very confusing. At one point, the auctioneer grasped her chin and forced her face up. Callie wasn't sure what was going on. She caught a glimpse of Porter. He looked very grim. And beside him, also dark-haired and brown and bearded, that had to be James. Callie felt another huge surge from her heart and her ears filled with a buzzing noise as she struggled to control her response again. The auctioneer dropped her chin and jerked Sienna's head up. He must have been showing them off.

Callie hoped that Sienna was cognizant enough to see Porter. There was no way to tell. Sienna gave no indication that she saw anything and the auctioneer dropped her face a second later.

Eventually, the auctioneer said something that sounded final, clapped his hands three times and gestured to the left. There were cheers and claps, but also some mutters and ugly shouts.

From his grand table, Emil smirked slightly. He raised his right hand, palm outward. That seemed to be some sort of indicator that the auction was over. Someone gestured off to the left and two men moved forward towards the stage area. Callie caught the movements out of the corner of her eye.

"Next we have..." Emil started. He never finished the sentence. There was a loud disturbance from the back of the room. "What is this?" Emil said impatiently. The doors began to shudder. They were thrown inward with a great deal of violence, knocking several men over as they sprang into the room. Beyond the doors, Callie saw men in combat gear, with large rifles. They had dark helmets with shields, gloves, vests, and everything else Callie had seen from news reports of soldiers. She hoped this was a good sign.

Then, back from where Callie and Sienna had come from, there was another, much louder disturbance. It was like a huge wave of black. All the other women, still in their burquas, came running out, shouting and causing a massive near-riot. They were pretty angry, as far as Callie would tell. They weren't saying anything she could understand. The tones were fairly unmistakable; they were flat-out pissed.

The two men who had moved forward quickly got to the stage. They passed Emil like shadows, and they were standing in front of Callie and Sienna before Callie could think to move away.

"Shh, Callie, love, it's all right. Don't do anything." Oh God, it was James. She couldn't comprehend it. He carefully helped her lay down, protecting her from the room with his own body. Dimly, she noticed that Porter was holding Sienna by the arms, speaking to her softly. Blankly, Sienna raised her tired face and stared for a second or two. Then, suddenly, like she came to life again, she screamed something and collapsed. Porter kept holding her. Callie had the distinct impression that he might never let her go again.

Not that she had any room to criticize; she'd latched onto James and was clutching his clothes so tightly that her knuckles were white. She realized that she was trembling violently again. In fact, she realized she was also crying.

The women who'd been freed were throwing shoes at whoever they were in range of. Several skittered across the stage, missing the four of them.

There was a great deal of disturbance happening beyond James' protecting body. Shouts and sounds of running and bodies hitting each other. There were several cracks of rifles, and the sounds slacked off somewhat. Someone was shouting something. Callie couldn't catch the words. It was too loud still.

"Shh, baby, don't cry." James whispered a little distracted.

"I can't help it!" Callie wailed. She really couldn't. She wanted to stop, but it was beyond her control.

"Oh, God." James sighed. He raised his heads slightly. "Mason, she's losing it."

"That's understandable, James." Callie heard Mason say from right above her. "You should have seen you fucking lose it earlier. That was something to see."

"It won't hurt her, will it?"

Mason snorted. "Of course not. She's very strong, as previously stated, multiple times. Just keep her warm. This is called shock. Callie, my dear, you will probably experience this type of thing for a while, and it can be scary, but it will lessen with time. Just don't suppress it too much."

Callie nodded, sort of.

Mason smiled slightly. He gave her a small drink from a bottle. "That should help a little."

"What is it?" James asked suspiciously.

"The alcohol we had last night. What did you fucking think?"

Mason moved over to check on Sienna. James still looked very worried. "Are you okay, Callie? Really?"

Callie began to calm somewhat. Drinking alcohol on an empty stomach felt like she had swallowed fire, but it spread quickly and she felt a bit more detached and manageable. "Yes, I think so."

"I am so sorry for all this."

"Like it was your fucking fault."

"Well, no, but still..."

"Oh, drop it, James. I imagine we will both have enough to be legitimately sorry for. Let's not borrow random other things." Callie giggled suddenly. "Sorry, James, but it is true."

James smiled. "You're right, of course."

"Good, now just hold me for a long time."

"How long?"

"How about we start with forever and move on from there?" Callie giggled again. She was just so glad to have him back with her that she couldn't seem to stop saying stupid things.

James laughed. "All right, I will! But you'll have to marry me for

154

that to work." He said as he wrapped her in his arms tightly.

Callie didn't really answer with words, but who needed words anyway? She kissed him, still crying. It was probably not the best kiss ever. Who cared? Mentally she made a note to say it out loud. Later of course. The sounds continued. It sounded like there was some serious chaos in the room. Orders were being shouted.

"Emil? Did he get away? Is he going to be arrested or something." Callie asked finally.

James snorted very softly. "Emil will be facing a very high judge. In fact, he is facing the highest judge, if I understand things like that correctly."

Callie pulled back slightly and looked up at James. "He is? Who?"

James smiled grimly. "God." Callie turned to look but James gently pulled her face back. "No, Callie. Don't look. I don't want it to upset you. It's not a pretty picture. Lots of blood."

"Oh. Then I won't look."

The shouting changed in tone. There were fewer women's voices now. Callie peeked out over James' shoulder. The dark vested soldiers were coming towards the stage, looking extremely competent. The leader hopped up on the stage and faced the room. The women covered in black were all against one wall, the rest of the room consisted to the former buyers. The leader of the soldiers raised his arm confidently. His soldiers were keeping the buyers from escaping. Callie was surprised to see that the women were standing quite calmly. She knew she was a mess of emotion.

"All right, gentlemen. You're all under arrest for crimes against humanity. The UN will be most interested to hear why you all managed to find yourselves in a slave sale without the slightest idea as to what was going on, as I am sure that is your defense. Start practicing your lies now."

The men out in the room glared and muttered angrily. Several shoes were hurled towards the stage. The UN soldier didn't even bother responding. He gestured sharply and his efficient soldiers began to

155

remove small groups of buyers to somewhere outside.

"Well, sir, did it go like you thought it would?" The soldier asked Mason quietly.

"I think so, yes. How many escaped?"

The soldier shrugged. "I can't really say. I haven't had a preliminary report yet. I think we can safely assume that we have most of them. One or two might have found a rat hole to run down."

Mason laughed. "I love that mental imagery."

"Feel free to use it. I probably read it somewhere. I tend to plagiarize rather freely."

"The best one-liners are like that. I hope that this area will not be able to unite under a single leader like Emil again for a long time. However, the government is going to have to step up a little on that end."

"You're right, of course. I understand that you might have some direct hand in making certain arrangements for that?"

Mason shrugged. "May have." He smiled evasively.

"Well, sir, you run a good mission. I hope to work with you and your group again sometime." The soldier shook hands with Mason and went off. He probably had something important to do.

Mason was surveying the room calmly. "Let's wait to go anywhere until the UN has who they want." He said softly.

"Of course, great leader." Porter said mockingly.

"Porter, if you don't quit with that I am going to kick your fucking ass."

"Like you fucking could."

"Don't tempt me. And don't make any bets, bitch." Mason paused. "Michael and Juan should be coming soon enough."

"Juan was here?" Callie asked.

"Of course he was, Callie. I couldn't send Michael into that alone. He would be ripping people apart. Juan can talk him down, sometimes."

"Oh. I'm glad. But I am also a little angry that you didn't tell us."

Mason sighed. "I understand, but you know why I had to do it that way."

156

"Yes. I'm still mad at you though."

"I'm glad you understand. I can live with people being mad at me."

Porter laughed. "Because you fucking deserve it."

"Fuck off."

Chapter 25

It took a while for the room to clear most of the way out. Michael and Juan lead Gabriella and Karen, both dressed in burquas up to the stage area.

"It went off the way it was supposed to, then, Mason?" Juan asked.

"More or less."

"Who got Emil?"

"You should really ask the old pirate that." Mason gestured towards Porter. "He may have had something to do with that."

Porter smiled, his eyes twinkling outrageously. "May have." He said.

Juan sighed loudly and rolled his eyes. "Damn it, Porter."

"It's a story for later, Johnny. Plus, I enjoy yanking your damn chain around."

"Fuck you. I want to know now."

"Too fucking bad."

Mason held up his hand. "It'll have to wait anyway. The UN commander is coming back."

They all waited as the soldier came back towards the stage, looking around him professionally. He didn't say anything to them, just waved his hand in farewell and left.

"That's it, then. We can go. Johnny, spring the locks."

"Ah, man. Why don't you have Porter do it? He's a better lock-pick."

"Because he's occupied. Just fucking do it, Juan. Bitch about it later."

"Fine. Jeez." Juan took a slender awl from his pocket and felt around inside the lock on Callie's shackles for a minute. "Yeah, okay, I have one that will work." He said, pulling a bunch of keys out and searching through them quickly. He put one into the lock, made some minute adjustments, the tapped it with the handle of his awl. The lock sprang open. He moved to do Sienna's.

"Where did he get the keys?" Callie asked.

Mason shrugged. "They're blanks. He printed them. We should probably clear out of here. Will you be able to walk, Callie?"

"Um, I don't know."

"Well, whatever, James can carry you. He wasn't hit too hard. Porter is the real question. As usual. You'd think, after all this time, he would be able to keep his damn self out of fucking trouble, but no."

"It gives you something to worry about, Mason." Porter noted.

"Yeah, that's exactly what I need." Mason considered Callie and Sienna for a moment. "Uh, yeah, do we have any clothes at all for these two?"

Callie blushed very red and pulled her blouse closed. Juan trotted off to look in the soldiers' quarters.

"It's not your fault, Callie." Mason said gently. "You are going to be very distracting if we take you out that way, though." He grinned at James. "Actually, I am a bit surprised that James has kept himself under control."

James laughed. "It hasn't been easy!"

Callie blushed even redder. "You're making fun of me, aren't you, Dr. Briggs?"

Mason shook his head. "No, Callie, I am not, not really. Why don't we go aside a little and talk about some things while Juan is looking for clothes?"

"Um, okay."

Porter shook his head, saying to James, "It's probably a good thing we don't know who put those bruises on her. I have another knife or two that need using."

"It's been taken care of, Porter." Michael said.

"Did you do it? How many were there?"

"No, and three, Emil didn't take to it nicely. He had the guys shot. We all had to watch. It was pretty fucking intense."

"Oh. I'll let it go."

"I won't tell the story til later. You two need to be far the fuck

159

away from here first."

"That bad?"

Michael nodded.

Mason Helped Callie down off the stage. "Can you walk, my dear, or should I carry you?"

"Um, I can walk, Dr. Briggs." Callie was still embarrassed. She wasn't the smallest person in the world.

Mason sighed. He seemed to know what she was thinking. "Callie, who ever told you that you were fat is fucking messed up. I might just send Porter, Michael, and Juan to educate them. You are no burden at all. Now, let me carry you before you fall over. And don't call me Dr. Briggs."

"Okay, Mason." Callie said in a small voice. "It's just…"

"I understand, Callie, but you have to get over the shit someone else has laid on you. It's not your shit. It's theirs. Don't go carrying around more shit than you need to."

Porter laughed. "You have such a way with words, Mason!"

Mason gave him a long, steady look as he picked up Callie. "Porter, do not even fucking start. Not right now."

Porter held up his hands in surrender. Mason took Callie to the far corner. "We can't go far, just in case something happens that I need to know about."

"I understand, Mason."

"All right." Mason set her down without showing exertion at all. "Let's have a seat here and talk. You are going to suffer from flashbacks, you know. I need to gauge how bad they might be, and also I need to know how to best help you."

Callie nodded. She was dreading this. Mason was her friend, though. Maybe it would be okay after all.

Mason continued, watching her closely. "Why don't you just tell me what you want to, for starters? How did you feel the first day?"

"Feel?" Somehow, Callie had been caught completely off-guard by that. "I felt…" How had she felt? It was something she hadn't thought about. Like at all. Mason kept watching her carefully. He seemed to really care about what she said. "I guess, well, I guess I felt scared." Mason didn't say anything. He kept watching her sympathetically, silently encouraging her to keep going. "I was really scared, Mason. I didn't know what to do pretty much the whole time. I felt like I was making it all up, but I never knew if I did it right." Suddenly, Callie began to shake again. She realized just how frightened she had been the whole time. It was a huge revelation. She should have been incapacitated by the fear. "Oh, Mason! I was so scared! What if I did it wrong? What if they killed me? Or, even worse, what if they killed Sienna because I did it wrong?"

Mason held her shoulders firmly. "Stop. Now. You did nothing wrong. Nothing. Do you hear me?" Callie nodded. She didn't believe him. Mason shook his head impatiently. "I mean it, Callie. Sienna is alive because you did everything exactly right. I know her pretty well. She is the closest I have ever seen her to a breakdown. Do you understand what I am saying right now? She is alive because of you. There is nothing else that kept her here. You did. You only. Understand?"

"But, Mason, I did it wrong. I know I did. I always do!"

"Callie, I am about this close to slapping you. Stop. Now. You did it right. What the hell else could you even fucking expect yourself to do?"

"Well..." Callie paused. She tried to think of something she might have done differently. She couldn't think of anything now. She had been so certain at the time that she was inadequate. "There must be something, right, Mason?" She asked, desperately.

"You have got to be fucking kidding me right now. You were stuck in a cell, neither of you with any sort of weapon or tools, and Sienna fucking about to lose her goddamn mind, and you are saying you should have... what? Busted the damn door down? You weigh something like 135 pounds, Callie. And what would you do against soldiers with fucking rifles? You did it right, exactly right."

Callie was dreadfully confused. She thought that she would have to make excuses for everything she'd done and defend her actions, not be defended.

Mason sighed. He gently turned her face towards him. "Callie, look at me. I don't know what shit you have been told about yourself, but I would never trust Sienna to anyone else."

"But she's so much better than me!" Callie whispered. Shit, she'd said it out loud. It was finally out.

Mason raised one eyebrow. "Ah, that's what this is, then. Sienna is a remarkable woman. But you know you can't live in her shadow. She doesn't want you there. You deserve to be out on your own. You did an amazing job. I think perhaps we shall continue this later. Juan is back, and I can see that Porter has something he wants to say." Mason helped Callie stand up and she leaned on his arm to get back. She still felt weak, too weak for much.

"How do you know Porter has something to say?"

"Because he is fucking waving at me with all the urgency of a toddler who has to fucking piss, that's how. Porter is not always very subtle, especially not with friends."

Callie laughed involuntarily. "He is so courteous though!"

"Well, of course he is, Callie. He is actually one of the most charitable people I know. Anyway, I want you to think long and hard on what I told you."

They reached the stage area in a minute or so. Porter had finally let Sienna go, and she was shakily pulling on a uniform shirt. Juan was helping her to button it. Callie wondered why Porter wasn't helping her; she got her answer as soon as she got to the stage. Porter leapt down lightly. He always was quick and balanced. Immediately he swept her up in an enormous hug.

"Oh, Callie, you wonderful beautiful woman! You kept her safe." His voice cracked and he swallowed the rest of what he was going to say.

Callie started crying again. Porter was shaking slightly. He was probably crying, too. When he finally set her down, Callie was a mess of conflicting emotions. Porter kissed her, bowed very low, and held out his arm to Sienna.

Juan grinned at him. "You are a fucking mess, you old pirate."

162

Porter nodded. "No shit, Johnny. What the fuck did you expect?"

"More of it, of course!"

"Fuck you, Johnny."

Juan shrugged. "Well, there is that option, I suppose."

Porter laughed. Mason smiled at Callie, his face clearly saying, "See?"

Juan also leapt off the stage. "Here, Callie. I know that shirt is ruined. Maybe this one will cover all the holes."

Michael shook his head despairingly. "No, Juan, it has the right amount of holes. If it covered all the holes, you should wear it."

Juan looked puzzled. "Uh, why me, Mikey?"

"Because then it would cover your fucking ugly mug over and we could still see Callie. She's way prettier."

"Ah, dammit, I didn't see that one coming."

"You should have."

"Yeah, yeah, whatever bitch." Juan carefully draped the shirt over Callie and helped her button it up. "This looks a lot less distracting. I think we will be okay outside. We'll still be obvious, but not aggressively so much."

"Then let's blow this joint." Mason said. "We've spent long enough in this hell-hole and it sounds like we have shit-loads of stories to tell."

Chapter 26

As they moved towards the doorway, Mason looked hard at Porter. "You are not even going to try and carry her the whole fucking way. You aren't up to it and I won't let you. Neither will Juan or Michael. Just give up now."

Porter sighed and rolled his eyes. "Fine, Mason. You can fucking win this round. Just because you are feeling all bitchy because you were worried."

"The worrying didn't stop, idiot. I'm still fucking worried. You keep acting like a fucking moron all the time."

"You just like being in control all the fucking time, bitch."

"You just like being a complete ass all the fucking time. Are you really going to make me force you?"

"No, I suppose not." Porter surrendered with bad grace.

"Good. I'll put her in good hands." Mason gestured to Michael. "It's just as well."

Sienna smiled weakly. "Anyone going to ask my opinion?"

"No. Not this time." Mason said gently. Porter shook his head, too.

Sienna laughed softly. "Oh, fine, you two. I'll ignore it this once."

Michael picked her up as easily as if she were a doll and they moved out into the bright sunlight. Callie hadn't expected there to be so much light and she squinted against the glare. Being inside for the last few days made her sensitive to the sun.

Mason glanced at her shrewdly. "How are you doing?" He asked softly.

Callie smiled suddenly. "It feels so good to be out and not going back. I don't think I can even explain it."

Mason nodded. "I am very glad to hear it."

James had to carry her most of the way. She just didn't have the energy to make it on her own, and now that she knew she could relax a little, it was easier to trust her friends to take care of anything that popped up. Mason seemed to know the way back pretty well. Plus, the
164

sun was starting to give her a headache. Maybe it was a lack of sleep, too. Something was definitely giving her a headache.

At one intersection of narrow streets, Mason paused. Looking significantly at Porter, he said, "Would you take them to the house? I have some business to take care of with the UN commander."

Porter smiled. "It had better include some lamb."

Juan looked as confused as Callie felt. "What the fuck does lamb have to do with anything?"

Porter grinned suddenly. "You'll see!"

"God damn it, Porter! I fucking hate that!"

"Too fucking bad. You do it to me all the time."

"Yes, but that is different."

"Oh, really?"

"Of course it is!" Juan said loftily. "I am around to knock you down a few notches. I thought you knew that."

"Yeah, that is definitely the only reason you are around."

"Well, that and to be awesome, of course. You all need more fucking awesome in your lives."

Callie was too tired to care where Mason had disappeared to. She just wanted to sleep. The fear of being in the cell made her wary of trying. She found she was afraid to sleep out here. If something happened, she had to be awake. Hopefully this feeling would go away, and soon.

Porter opened the door of a nondescript house and they all went in. James, who was a lot more observant than she thought, said softly, "I think she needs sleep."

Porter nodded seriously. "Of course she does. I have some experience in this type of thing, James; she shouldn't be alone. Either we can put Sienna and the other ladies in with her, or you can be there, but she shouldn't be alone."

"Now, Porter, that's not much of a choice. You know I won't let her be alone."

"Well I would fucking hope not."

"Give me some credit, please."

"Like I said, I hoped you wouldn't be a fucking idiot, but one never knows."

James grinned. "I can be a fucking idiot anyway, just not on this topic."

Porter laughed. "We are all fucking idiots. You can have the room we slept it. I will take Sienna to the other one. Johnny and Mikey can fucking fend for themselves; there are a few other rooms for them." He winked outrageously. "I am no more an idiot than you are."

James breezed through the front rooms quickly. Callie had a confused memory of smallish rooms with little furniture. Then they were in a cool, dark back room. There were beds along all the walls. They weren't very big, but she didn't much care. It looked like luxury compared to where she had been.

"Is there anything you need?" James asked her gently.

"Could I take a bath or something first? I feel so dirty."

"Of course. Let me get it set up for you." He left quickly and Callie heard water running somewhere. Karen appeared in the doorway. She swiftly closed the door and came to help Callie unbutton the shirt.

"Thanks, Karen." Callie sighed. She looked down at her dirty and torn clothes. "I guess I had better keep these to put back on."

"Like hell." Karen said firmly. "I have some extra clothes. You're close enough to my size. I know exactly how hard it is to wear things that have bad memories attached to them."

Callie stared at her. "Are you sure?"

Karen nodded. "Very sure. Just give me those ruined clothes. You can drape the one shirt over you like a robe and I will bring you the rest."

"Thanks. Really." Callie sniffed loudly. She started to take off her shirt and skirt.

"You are welcome, Callie. Let me get those for you. But I am afraid that I don't have a bra that will fit you. You're a lot tinier in the ribcage than I am."

Callie smiled. "That's okay. I don't mind not wearing restrictive things sometimes."

Karen laughed. "I'll be back in a minute or two." She closed the door behind her and Callie did as she suggested, putting the other shirt on like a robe. It was pretty short for a robe, but who the hell was going to care? She sat on the bed and waited. It felt very nice to know she would be getting clean and sleep. There was a tap on the door and Karen came back in with some clothes folded up in a pile which she set on the bed.

"Let's get you to the bath now. James has filled it for you and Porter is getting some food together."

"Okay." Callie said wearily. It seemed very hard to stand up and walk anywhere. "I hope it isn't very far."

Karen smiled. "It doesn't matter; I am going to help you, and Gabriella will bring the clothes. Don't argue about it. We want to help you."

"Okay, okay. I won't argue."

"Besides, we have Sienna after you."

"Oh, yeah, I should get going then."

"You can't always put her first, Callie. I know that it sometimes seems selfish to take time for yourself, and I am working on that, too. But you need to take care of you right now. Sienna wants that, and you need it."

Callie just kind of nodded. It seemed too hard to think about right now. Karen led her slowly to the bathroom and shut the door. The bathtub wasn't large or deep, but Callie didn't care in the slightest.

"Ah. I feel like I have died and gone to Heaven right now." She murmured as she lay back in the water.

Karen smiled. "Pretty crappy heaven if this is all there is."

"I am not complaining."

"Do you want me to wash your hair for you?"

"Oh my God, that would be amazing."

After telling her to take all the time she needed, Karen left Callie alone. Just lying in the water and letting her mind drift was beautiful.

Callie wasn't sure how long she was in the bath, but the water was definitely cool by the time she roused herself. Karen had left a towel within easy reach. Callie stood up and let the water and dirt run out. She felt like new, except that she was still very tired.

There was tap at the door and Karen came back in, Gabriella behind her with the clothes. They both helped Callie get dressed and then they assisted her to the kitchen area.

Porter had put some food out. Sienna was at the table. Karen and Gabriella helped Callie sit, then they helped Sienna out. Porter smiled at Callie. "Feel better?"

"You have no fucking idea."

He pushed a plate towards her. "You probably need to eat, but I am guessing you won't want much. Try some of this. And have some water."

"I feel a little helpless. Everybody is doing such nice stuff for me, and I am just taking it all." Callie said ruefully.

Porter sat across from her and covered her small hands with his long sensitive ones. "Is that really what you think? We aren't doing anything because we want to be nice; we're doing it because we love you and you scared us all shitless."

Callie stared at him. "Well, I guess I know that, but…"

Porter smiled slightly. "Callie, you are talking to the king of self-loathing. I am getting better though. So here's what I am telling you: we love you and none of this is a burden for any of us. Making food and helping you get dressed is nothing compared to the fucking shit we pulled to get you out, so don't cheapen it for us, okay?"

Callie looked down, embarrassed. "Um, okay."

Porter tilted her chin up again. "Look at me for a second. I am serious, Callie. I admit that sometimes love is annoying as hell and feels like a real chore. But without it, we're just fucking empty shells faking the motions. We all want you to feel special, not because we have to or because Mason told us to, but because we love you. Love takes the burden and makes it bearable. That's what I mean by you not being a

168

burden. And be a little fucking selfish, girl! You deserve it!"

Callie felt a little self-conscious. She glanced back down. Porter seemed so earnest though, so she said, "Okay, Porter. I will try."

Porter laughed. "Good enough. Now eat something and you can go sleep after that, I promise."

Callie laughed in spite of herself. "I will, I will."

"Good!" Porter stood up again and went back to the sink area.

Callie ate some of the bread with something tangy and sweet on it and drank water. She was very close to drowsing again when Karen and Gabriella brought Sienna back in.

Porter looked at Sienna quickly, then he left the kitchen. Karen and Gabriella also left.

Sienna sighed. "Oh my God. I never thought I would be clean again."

Callie smiled slightly. "Me, too."

Sienna looked at Callie for a long moment. "Callie, my dear, you are amazing. I will never be able to say 'thank you' enough."

Callie blushed. "It's fine, Sienna."

"No, my dear. You don't quite believe me. I can almost always tell when someone is lying to my face. I really mean it. Thank you. I thought I had lost everything. You helped me. I could never have done it without you. I was lost, and you helped lead me back."

"Sienna, I didn't do anything like that! All I did was..."

"Callie, you seem to think you aren't good enough. Why?"

"Um, well, see..." Callie floundered. She hadn't been prepared for this, not at all. "It's just that, well, you and Porter..."

Sienna sighed and shook her head. "Callie, really. Did you know that James was worried about introducing you to us?"

"He was?"

"Of course. He didn't want you to feel jealous or embarrassed. He probably never told you any of this, but he was so anxious to show you off that he almost cried when he broached the subject with Porter."

"He did not!"

169

Sienna smiled at her. "He did. Porter was sensitive to that and all. But here's the thing: James has never been interested in me at all. I can usually tell that sort of thing, too. I've had men and women chasing me for a long time. After a while, it becomes almost second-nature to fend off. I never had to do anything like that with James. Never. And I don't fucking lie about shit like that."

"No! I know you don't. It is just...surprising or something."

"Perhaps it is, at that. James always went for redheads." Sienna grinned suddenly. "I make a shitty redhead!"

Callie laughed in spite of herself. "Okay! I will try to get better."

"Do, please. I am in awe of how you have acted these last few days. Absolutely in awe."

Porter and James came back in quietly. Porter looked at the two of them at the table, his eyes twinkling. "Have you two done whatever it was that you needed to do now? Would you like to sleep?"

Sienna sighed with a great deal of dramatic emphasis. "I suppose. Take me to bed, now."

Porter bowed mockingly. "As my lady commands!"

Callie smiled. "Did you two plan all this or something?"

Porter smiled as he carefully picked Sienna up. "No, Callie. I knew Sienna had something to say, but she never discussed it with me and we didn't plan it out. I know her pretty well by now."

Sienna snuggled into him. "Get to know me better. And James, don't come knocking unless you want to join."

James blushed furiously. "Of course not!"

Sienna laughed. "Only joking, James. Now then, Porter, I am tired. Let's go sleep."

Chapter 27

James came over to Callie. "I know you are tired, so let's not argue about if you need to sleep right now. I'll take you to bed and we can argue about it later."

Callie smiled and was taken over by an enormous yawn. "That sounds like a good plan to me."

He picked her up gently. "I can walk, James." Callie protested.

"That is just too bad because I won't let you."

Callie remembered what Mason had said a little earlier. "Okay." She sighed. It was probably easier to just give it up than to argue and look stupid when it happened anyway.

"Thank you." He carried her back to the dark room.

Callie sighed softly. "I am really tired. I hope I sleep."

James helped her to a bed. "I'll be here, for as long as you need me to be."

Callie suddenly pulled his hand down, forcing him very close to her. She pulled herself up slightly and kissed him as hard as she could. James seemed a little surprised. He quickly got over that. Perhaps being tired made her impulsive; she wasn't sure. It didn't really matter. Callie didn't feel like being reserved and proper. She wanted to show James how she felt and at the same time get closer to him. That desire was very strong.

"Callie, baby, you need to sleep. And I can't do this right now. I'm sorry. That wouldn't be right." James whispered as he pulled back.

"I know, but..."

"No, Callie, not right now."

"Dammit, James, why do you have to be so rational?" She accused.

He smiled at her. "I said I was sorry."

She snorted and turned onto her side away from him. "Not sorry enough."

"Baby, please..." James was actually begging. "I can't take advantage of you."

Callie didn't answer. She knew she was being unfair. She knew she was being ridiculous. She still didn't want to give it up. The feeling of having control and power was rewarding right now. Then, with a sigh, she gave in. The power, she decided, wasn't worth hurting somebody she wanted to love. Rolling back to face him, she said, "I know. I was being stupid."

"No, not stupid. Just difficult."

She smiled. "Okay, difficult. You are right. I should sleep."

"Do you want to be alone?"

"No. I want you to be right here."

"Will you be good?" James asked with a slight smile.

"Why don't you find out? I bet when I am bad, I am really, really good."

James laughed. "You are impossible."

"And you like it."

"Of course I do. I like this new you. It suits you better than the old one. You're more authentic this way."

Callie didn't say anything to that. Could she have changed that much in just a few days? Really? She yawned. She'd have to think about it later. Sleep now. James was lying beside her, and his warmth made her suddenly feel very vulnerable.

"Don't go anywhere." She said sleepily.

"Of course not, Callie."

She drifted off into vague dreams that she didn't remember when she woke back up. Gradually, she heard soft voices coming from the other parts of the house. She lay for a while listening. It sounded like Mason and Porter and maybe someone else. James was still beside her. He hadn't left. She felt a little glad of that. He stirred when she sat up.

"Is it time to get up then?" He asked groggily.

"Probably. I think Mason is back." Callie stretched. "How long did I sleep, anyway?"

"About two hours." James stood up. "I wonder if there is any food in this place."

172

"Food?"

"Aren't you hungry? I'm really hungry. Haven't eaten since this morning, and then only because Porter and Mason made me."

Callie thought about it. Once she did, she realized how hungry she was. The stress of the cell and the small amounts of food had caused her to unconsciously suppress her feelings of hunger. "I think I am going to starve right here and now." She said with deliberate overemphasis.

"Uh-huh." James teased her.

"Shut up and take me to the food."

"As my lady commands." He bowed mockingly.

"You spend way too much time with Porter." She said.

"No kidding? I never would have guessed."

Callie laughed. It was too hard to pretend to be upset with him. Together they walked into the kitchen. Porter was there with Mason. They were doing things at the counters and trading insults. It was perfectly normal.

Callie sat at the table. Mason glanced up and nudged Porter. "Plate, slave."

"Yes, Exalted Master." Porter bowed extravagantly and brought Callie a small plate with figs and bread on it. "You'll have to wait until the rest is done, I am afraid. This should be enough to start with, though."

"Thank you."

"I live but to serve, Lady!"

Callie laughed at him. "You are incorrigible!"

Mason nodded vigorously. "The lady is a prophet. Notice how she speaks the truth."

Porter went back by Mason, casually slapping him upside the head. "Shut the fuck up."

Mason hit him back. "You shut up." He washed his hands and came over to the table drying them.

Porter looked outraged. "Hey, who said you were done?"

"I did. Besides, you are too much of a fucking control freak to let me help more than that."

173

"Yeah, okay, you are probably right." Porter turned back and started doing things again.

Mason looked at Callie. "How are you doing?"

"Better, thank you."

"Good." Mason reached into a pocket and handed something to James. "For later." He said. James looked in the packet and nodded. "Now, Callie," Mason continued as if nothing had happened. "When everyone else gets back out here, we'll probably have to rehash the whole damn story. We do that a lot, with lots of fucking additions from everybody. I want you to let me know if it is too much for you at any point."

"Okay, Mason. I promise I will."

Mason nodded. "All right. I will hold you to it. "

Callie looked curiously at Porter's back. He seemed pretty intent on what he was doing. "What's Porter doing?"

Mason smiled. "Cooking, of course. What the fuck else would he be doing? He has to keep his well-honed knife skills and fucking bristly as hell personality."

Callie giggled, then felt a little guilty. Porter didn't even turn around. "Mason, you are just so damn cute. Come over here so I can knock some of it out of you." He didn't sound upset at all.

"Fuck you." Mason said pleasantly.

Callie hurridly broke in. "What? I mean, what are you making?"

"Lamb. Mason finally got something fucking right."

Mason rolled his eyes. "If you don't tell me what the fuck to get, you end up with what I want, Porter. You should fucking know better by now."

"Oh, I know better, bitch."

"Whatever. The way you bitch and moan about it all makes me think I won't expend the fucking effort next time."

"Good, because then I won't feel obligated to fucking make anything."

"Listen, ass, you were just bitching last fucking night that you

174

didn't have anything to cook with!"

"Yeah, well, that was last night."

Mason threw up his hands in mock exasperation. "I fucking give up!" He grinned and winked at Callie.

"I don't always know when you two are joking." She confessed.

"Oh, that part is easy." Porter said easily. "If we're talking, we're almost always joking."

"Pretty much." Mason agreed. "It's almost never easier to joke about shit than be serious. That's one of the reasons we do it."

"That doesn't make sense, Dr. Briggs!" Callie protested.

"Doesn't it, though? Is it easier to be offended, or easier to laugh at yourself?"

"Um... Offended, I guess."

"Is it easier to joke about making a mistake, or become angry about it?"

"Angry?"

"And lastly, Callie, is it easier to make fun of yourself, or is it easier to be afraid that everyone is laughing at you?" Mason was looking at her very hard now. He knew.

Callie blushed very red. She hung her head. Mason put his hand on her shoulder gently. "Look, Callie, I am not accusing you. Someone has fucked you over. It might be you, but after what I have seen of you these last few days, I don't think so. Perhaps, sometime soon, we will have to try and figure out what has happened to you." He glanced at Porter, who had stopped and was watching them. "However, I think I will talk to you about it alone. Porter isn't that balanced and he sometimes takes things into his own hands."

Porter held up his hands in a gesture of surrender. "Sorry, Mason. I get fucking angry when someone hurts somebody I love."

"You're supposed to get angry, idiot. I want you to be fucking moderate about it though. That part you lack sometimes."

"I know, I know. It's just... Callie has been an amazing woman, before and all through, and if someone fucked her over, it makes my blood boil. I will bow to your expertise, however."

"Good. About fucking time."

Chapter 28

Later, when everyone made it to the kitchen area, possibly lured by the delicious smells of the dishes Porter had finished, the small room was quite cozy. Callie found that a little unnerving. She'd been in a small cell with just Sienna in it, and Sienna hadn't been interacting for a good amount of it. All this boisterousness and jocularity was almost more than she could handle. She wasn't always comfortable with crowds and this room was almost crowded.

Mason smiled at her. "Are you all right so far?"

"Well, this is a lot of people." Callie hedged.

"I know, but they want you here. And it is good for you, too."

Callie nodded. She'd just have to suck it up and deal. Besides, they were all her friends. They'd all sacrificed an awful lot to get her out. She should at least pretend to be grateful and answer questions if they had them. Actually, she was intensely grateful; she just was feeling overwhelmed by all the happiness and camaraderie in the room right now.

"Yo, Porter! When did you learn to make such fantastic shit?" Juan asked enthusiastically. "And what is this fantastic shit, anyway?"

"I made it the fuck up and it is lamb."

"Damn! I think I could raise a whole damn flock if you would promise to cook them for me."

"There might be some problems with that."

Juan shrugged. He and Michael were wolfing food at a surprising rate. Callie tried the lamb, which was spicy and sweet at the same time. It was really good. It just seemed a little rich for her right now. Porter must have read her mind. He passed her a plate with only fruit and bread on it with a wink. Callie smiled at him. He always knew.

Sienna was quiet, as well. She still looked pale and tired. Porter also hounded her to eat.

"My dear, leave me the fuck alone!" She said at one point. "I am not hungry right now."

"Too bad for you." Porter said dispassionately. He got up and returned with two glasses full of something. He gave one to Callie and put one by Sienna. "And you are going to fucking drink it all."

"Fine. Then you had better fucking leave me alone." Sienna retorted.

"Deal." Porter nodded.

Mason grinned at them. "Aw, isn't that cute, Mikey? They are an old married couple already!"

Michael hadn't expected that and choked, laughing. "Damn, Mason! Not when I am fucking eating!"

"You're always fucking eating."

"Yeah!" Juan noted. "Mason would never say anything if we waited for you to be done eating!"

"As if that is a bad thing, Johnny." Michael said, reaching for more lamb.

Mason put up his hands in a gesture of defeat as everyone else laughed. Callie took a cautious sip from her cup. It was milk, but not cow milk. There was a wild taste to it. She knew James and Porter would hound her until she finished it, so she drank it all. Porter watched her, smiling as she set the cup down.

"What is this?" Callie asked.

"Camel's milk. You and Sienna need the calories and protein to help you recover."

"Camel?"

"You heard me."

"How do they milk a camel?"

"How the fuck should I know?"

Juan laughed merrily. "They go up and ask the camel very nicely."

Porter shook his head. "No, Johnny, I doubt that is any part of the process."

"It should be."

Michael threw an arm around Juan, covering his mouth from the other side and rendering him effectively motionless at the same time. Without any evidence of effort, he held him while Juan squirmed and wriggled to get free. "Any more of that, Porter?"

Porter shook his head. "No, sorry, Mikey. It was too fucking expensive. I know you like milk, but I didn't have that much on me and I didn't want to be tagged as a thief."

"Ah, well, sucks to be me." Michael said, releasing Juan calmly.

"You big gorilla! You about strangled me!" Juan accused, his face red from effort.

Michael shrugged. "I wanted to ask a question and you were too fucking loud anyway."

Gabriella and Karen were laughing. Gabriella looked at Juan very innocently. "I told you that you should moderate your voice."

"You're not helping."

"I'm not trying to."

"Then you are succeeding very well, damn it. How come everybody is against me, anyway?"

"Because you can take it." Mason shrugged.

"Great."

Once the food was gone and the table cleared, Porter brought out the card deck he seemed to always have with him. Looking around the table, he made a mental count. "Hm, there are too many here for standard parlor games. Not enough cards in the damn deck to deal out."

"Why not do something else, then?" Mason suggested, putting two bottles of alcohol out on the table.

"I like standard games, Mason. I don't have to explain rules. Fortunately, I have a spare." With an excessively theatrical gesture, he produced another deck.

Mason laughed. "Of course you have a spare. Why the fuck wouldn't you?"

"Precisely." Porter smiled as he began to shuffle the two decks together.

Juan accepted his cards and glanced at them. "How the hell did you keep these even with all the shit that went down? Dunno about anybody else, but two decks of cards are not the things I would be protecting if the shit hit the fan for me."

"It's three."

"The fuck?"

"Three decks, actually."

"Of course it is. And why do you have three decks on your person?"

Porter shrugged. "It's not too complicated, Johnny. Mason brought me my knives, and there is one deck in that bag, too. I tend to not use it with other decks, as the cards are slightly smaller."

"Oh, right. I had forgotten the knives."

Callie looked at her hand. It wasn't very good. "What knives?" She asked. That was a lot more interesting than her cards anyway.

"The ones Mason went and got from the house for me." Porter was frowning at his own hand, but it was probably a fake-out.

"You asked him to get knives?"

Mason smiled. "No, Callie, he didn't have to. I knew Porter would want something to avenge himself with. Since you all flew commercial aircraft, he wouldn't have them with him at Mahmoud's anyway."

"Oh. That makes sense."

After about a half hour of cards, Juan threw his hand in and leaned back. "Okay, fucking spill it. I want details. All of them. Right now. What the fuck really happened, Porter?"

"Didn't you hear the fucking memory shit Mason put us through?"

"Yes, I was there for that, but I don't want that. I want the shit, Porter."

Porter sighed. He gathered all the cards back and looked at them absently as he shuffled and cut them over and over. "It was terrible, Johnny. You have no fucking idea how bad it was. I felt weak and helpless. I can't stand that."

Juan nodded. "Yeah, that would do it to me, too."

"That's why I had to call Mason as soon as I could. Had to get somebody here."

James looked up. "How quick did you call?"

Porter squinted at the ceiling. "Uh, let's see."

"You said it had been about ten minutes at most." Mason said quietly.

"Then that's your answer."

"Damn." James said, shaking his head.

"Hey, I know when I am fucked and need help."

"Sometimes." Mason said gently.

Michael looked at Sienna. "How long did you two have to be in the cell?"

Sienna smiled slightly. "No, Michael, you shouldn't ask me. I have no clear memories of most of it. Callie is the one who did it all."

Callie was alarmed to see everyone looking at her. She hated being the center of attention. "Oh! Um, a couple of hours in the truck. Then Emil pulled us out and we were standing around for a while. I think I passed out once. Then they gave us water and put us in the cell."

"You passed out?" Michael asked, suddenly very angry.

"Um, yes. I think I got too hot?"

Juan smiled at her. "He's not mad at you, Callie. He's fucking pissed that it happened to you."

"Oh. That is a relief."

Mason gave Michael a hard look. "And if he doesn't fucking get it under control, right now, he is going to leave."

Michael took a deep breath and let it out. He loosened his large fist. "Yeah, okay. I am okay, Mason. Don't get pissy."

"Besides," Callie said hurriedly. "Nothing really happened in the cell, except that one thing."

James took her hand gently. Porter looked at her gravely. "That would be the one thing that put bruises all over you and a couple on my wife, I am assuming."

"Um, yeah. That thing." Callie mumbled and looked at the table quickly. She didn't want to relive any of that.

Fortunately, Michael and Juan took over. "We were doing the breakfast run after morning prayers." Juan said. "We saw that the door to their cell, way the hell at the end, was ajar. Not at all normal. So we and the commander dude ran down there as fast as we could. Gorilla, here, got in first, mostly because he pretty much plowed the commander out of the way."

Michael shrugged. "I didn't even notice. I knew some shit was going down, and I will be fucked if it goes down when I can fucking stop it."

"And what shit was that?" Mason asked.

"There were three guys in there trying to rape them."

Porter slammed his hand on the table, suddenly murderously livid. It made all the glasses and bottles jump. "Fucking hell!"

"I told you that you needed to be far away to hear it."

"I hope to hell you took fucking steps."

"What the fuck do you think, Porter? I think I broke the nose of the one holding Callie up against the wall. I hit him hard enough. Then Emil had them dragged out, strung up, and shot. The entire garrison had to watch, too. Fucking messed up."

James was still holding Callie's hand, but his was trembling now.

Porter closed his eyes for a moment. He opened them and reached a hand to Michael in silent gratitude. Michael took it for a second. Porter then extended it to Juan.

"Well. Judging from how I just lost my temper, I guess it's probably a good thing I didn't know about that sooner."

Michael smiled slightly. "Come on, Porter. I wouldn't tell you shit like that when it wouldn't do any fucking good."

"True. Thank you. Thank you both."

"So what happened to Emil? UN get him?"

Porter shook his head. "No, James and I had to walk in front of him to get to the stage area. I slipped him a nice going-away present as I passed. Fucking sent him off. I should probably ask for absolution about it though."

"Don't you have to feel guilty to get absolution?" Juan asked, sounding a bit skeptical.

"I do feel guilty about it, Juan."

"Oh. I am not all up on all that still."

Mason looked at Karen and Gabriella. "And how did it go in the other pen?"

Karen smiled. "We didn't have to work too hard, Mason. A lot of those ladies were already angry."

"I had hoped so, but it was a gamble."

Gabriella shrugged. "We knew that going in, Mason. It paid off in spades for us all."

"Amen, sister!" Mason raised his glass. Everyone else followed suit and they drank a toast.

Porter began to deal again. "I'm done with this shit. Let's play."

"One second." James said, putting his cards down. He took out the little packet Mason had given him earlier. Unwrapping it, he held a small gold circle with a small diamond on it out to Callie. "Callie, baby, would you marry me? I promise to get a better one later."

"Of course, James!" Callie smiled. She took the ring and put it on. She smiled at Mason and then at James, feeling a little teary and happy all at once.

"Hope it fits." Mason said. "It was kind of a toss-up."

"It will be just fine. Thank you, Mason!"

Mason shrugged. "It was the least I could do."

Porter smiled. "Which is why you did it twice, right?" He handed another ring to Sienna. "Just until I can make you another."

Sienna smiled. Tears started to run down her cheeks. She threw her arms around Porter and they kissed each other like there weren't seven other people in the room. Callie felt self-conscious about that. She wasn't quite sure what to feel.

It didn't last very long, then everyone started playing cards again like nothing had happened out of the ordinary. Callie noticed that both Porter's and Mason's eyes were very bright, though. As she picked up her own cards, her left hand felt a little different. She glanced up at Sienna and found she was looking right at her. Sienna smiled and winked. And Callie suddenly understood. She leaned over and kissed James very hard.

Chapter 29

Mason looked at his watch after a few hours. "All right, ladies and gentlemen, we have a flight out of here in a couple of hours. Let's get to it and we can sleep on the plane."

They all stood up and started to get ready to leave. Callie and Sienna, having nothing to pack up, sat at the table.

Sienna smiled and moved closer to Callie. "How does it feel?"

Callie smiled back. "Good. But I have to admit, I am a little scared."

"Scared of what?"

"Well, I am kind of scared to tell my parents. They have some friends that won't approve."

"That can be hard."

Callie hesitated before she asked, "Do you think I will have bad nightmares and stuff?"

"That will depend on you, really, Callie. Some people have horrible nightmares all the time, like Porter. Some have hardly any, like Juan. Personally, I think it might be a difference in temperament to account for some of that."

"There must be more to it than just that!" Callie protested.

"You're probably right. I think some of it has to do with what a person has gone through. I probably won't have terrible dreams about being in the cell, mostly because I don't really remember any of it. I will have fucking awful dreams about Mahmoud's office though. I already have. It was that place that gives me the worst dreams."

"I'm just scared of it all, now."

Sienna sighed. "I wish I could tell you the fool-proof way to make it stop, but there isn't one. If it gets too bad, Mason can give you some sleep aids, but they are no magic bullet."

Callie nodded sadly. "I know."

Sienna looked at her for a minute or two. "Callie, may I ask you a direct question?"

"Um, I suppose so."

185

"Why do you think you aren't good enough?"

Callie blushed. She stuttered for a minute before she finally managed to get out, "I guess I have never been good enough."

"Bull shit." Sienna said firmly. "You have always been good enough. Who told you that?"

"I don't think anyone really told me, Sienna. When my parents sent me to the prep school, there were some girls there who were from old money families and they were the popular ones. I guess I just assumed that they were right. They always talked about how money was the most important thing a family could have. They would get presents from home a lot, and when their parents came, they were always so stiff and proper with everyone. It was kind of hard; I thought that was what people were supposed to do. My parents acted afraid of them. Well, maybe not afraid, but careful around them, and I guess I just thought that was the thing to do."

"Money is such a poison." Sienna said. "It makes people think they are more important than those without it."

"Well, anyway, I just got used to deferring to people like that."

"Callie, you have to stop that. People only have the power you give them, you know. Besides, I know exactly what you are talking about. I know what it feels like to assume helplessness because a person is penniless. And I understand your feelings, but I also know you will have to overcome it all on your own. We, your friends, can help you, but we can't do it for you."

"I know, Sienna." Callie sighed. "I just wish that it could go away all of a sudden."

"We all wish that about the things that are hardest to change."

"Surely you don't."

"I most certainly do. You think it was easy to accept that Porter may never be able to marry me? And keep my virginity anyway? That temptation is very strong for me. Every once in a while, I wanted to say, 'Fuck it' and throw it all. I still do. But I have to steel myself against that. I repeat why I am doing what I am, and it helps me remember.

Understand, I am not saying that is the same as what you are going through. We all go through certain things, and each of us has different problems and ways to overcome those."

"Do you think it will ever go away?"

Sienna considered, staring out the window. "No, probably not. I think it has to do with who we are, and taking it away completely would change who we are."

"I was afraid of that."

Sienna smiled. "It does get easier, at least."

"Thank God for that."

Mason came out with several bags. "Ready, ladies?"

"How far is it?" Callie asked nervously. She knew she probably still couldn't get far on her own.

"The cab is right outside."

"Oh. I can probably get there, then."

"Let's get going. The sooner we are out of here, the better."

The cab ride was uneventful. It was so uneventful that Callie dozed off several times. She finally felt secure enough to nod off, and it was very nice. Every time she jerked awake, though, it was to a sense of profound dread. Her heart hammered frantically until she realized where she was and who she was with.

She was dozing when they got to the airport and she only woke up after everyone but Mason had left the cab. Callie jerked awake again, her brain trying to convince her that something terrible was happening. Mason gave her an appraising look.

"Goddamn it. I hope this stops soon." Callie mumbled.

Mason smiled. "It's hard to say, exactly, but it probably will." He extended a hand to help her stand up. "Shall we? Our plane is waiting."

"I suppose." Callie felt very slow, like her brain was stuffed with cotton or something. Sound seemed a bit muffled and she hardly registered anything happening around her.

Somehow, she made it onto the plane although she wasn't sure how that had happened. She was drowsing already by the time James made it to the seat beside her.

"Just make sure her seat belt is buckled and let her sleep." She heard Mason say and that was all she remembered for a long time.

Once, during the flight, the jet hit some heavy turbulence and jerked violently for a few minutes. Waking to the violent bouncing of the jet completely disoriented Callie and she was jostled for a while before she was able to gather herself.

"That was invigorating." She heard Porter say laconically from somewhere behind her seat.

"Oh, shut the fuck up, Porter. He's doing what he can." Mason responded, also behind Callie.

"I know he is, but that was pretty bad."

"Whatever. Have you considered what I told you yesterday?"

"Which part, the shrinking part, the not coloring my hair part, the being a fucking moron part, or something else?"

"Hey, you fucking listened! No, none of that. The part where I think somebody arranged that hit."

"Oh, that. Yeah, I did think about it a little, but, Mason, I am pulling a huge fucking blank on who might do that. I really am."

"Damn. I am, too. I don't like this though. Once we're back, I am going for more fucking information."

"Don't stir up a hornet's nest."

Mason snorted. "I'll fucking stir up a goddamn shark frenzy if I have to. You're not going to get hurt on my fucking watch, you hear me? Do you even know what that would do to your friends? Fucking destroy us. I speak from fucking hard experience, remember."

"No, I hadn't considered that."

"Do, idiot. Consider it fucking long and hard. And you are staying at home until I get this shit figured out, or else at a safe location."

"I have to work, Mason!" Porter protested. "You know I will go fucking stir-crazy stuck inside."

"Okay, you may go to work, but only if Michael or Juan is there with you and James. I don't want you in the front where just anyone can fucking see you. Let's not make you two targets again. I mean it. You are far too important to us. Do not even try to fucking argue with me."

Porter sighed. "Fine, whatever makes you fucking happy."

"None of this makes me happy, but that makes me a bit more secure about it all."

The voices stopped for a while and Callie considered what they had been talking about until she began to get sleepy again. She'd have to ask what it meant later.

Chapter 30

Once they landed, Callie woke up to Mason shaking her shoulder. "What?"

"You need to get up. James and Juan are going to take you home. Callie, this is very important: you have to stay with someone. You can stay at my house, Juan's, or Michael's, or James' apartment, but you must be with someone. I feel like there is more to this whole fucking story, and I will find out what it is."

"But, well, okay." Callie gave up.

"What? I want to know what you are thinking, please. I can't fucking do this blind."

"Well, um, are you sure you can take care of it? Um, that didn't come out right."

"Yes, I know what you mean. Yes, I think I can take care of it, but I need time to do it in. That's why you have to be safe, and these two fucking idiots have to be with you or at home." Mason gestured towards Porter and James. "They're supposed to be dead or something, and if they are not, that could complicate things. Does that make sense?"

Callie nodded slowly. "Yes, I suppose it does. I guess, as long as I won't be a bother, I can stay wherever."

"This is no bother, Callie. Why don't you and James stay at my house for a little while? I don't have any trouble keeping guests, and I also don't have any trouble being out of the way. We'll arrange clothes for you later."

"Okay, Mason." It was just too much to argue about now. Mason looked at her sharply. Callie braced herself; he always knew when she was just giving up without a fight.

"Callie..."

"I know, Mason. I do. I'm too tired to care and what you said makes sense, even if it annoys me."

"Good."

Porter was passing and looked surprised. "Good? What the hell is that supposed to mean?"

"It's good that she is annoyed at me. I am giving orders that will further complicate her life at a time when she wants less stress. Better than bottling it up."

"Oh. Yeah, I guess that is good, then."

"You should be fucking glad I didn't offer your house."

"You should be fucking glad that you didn't, too."

Mason grinned broadly. "It's your goddamned honeymoon, fucking moron. You better take care of business and I don't mean sleep."

Porter blushed furiously. Callie was a little surprised. She hadn't gotten used to the fact that Porter could experience such discomfort when Mason said things. Porter winked at Callie even though his face was still very red. "He brings out the worst in me, doesn't he?"

"I suppose."

Porter shot a nasty look at Mason, who was still grinning. "Bitch. I will get you for that."

"Yeah, whatever. Unless the house is on fire, I think you are going to be rather occupied for a long time, friend of mine."

"I'll make time to get you back."

"Like hell you will; I think you underestimate your lady."

Porter flushed again. "Dammit, Mason. Please stop."

Mason shrugged. "All right. We'll see you two later, Porter. She needs you. Maybe tomorrow night?"

"Sounds good. Your house?"

"Probably best."

"See you then." They shook hands and Porter left.

"How come he gets so upset?" Callie asked.

"Because he's uncomfortable with who he is. Everyone is. That's why we get embarrassed or upset by certain situations where we are unsure what is expected or where we don't feel comfortable with ourselves. Are you ready to go?"

Callie sighed. "I suppose so. But really, why is Porter upset by you teasing him about sex?"

Mason smiled slightly. "Because he thinks he isn't good enough.

191

Come now, Callie, you should be well-acquainted with that particular idea."

Callie looked away quickly. "Oh." She tried to stand up.

Mason sighed. "Here, please let me help you."

"But…"

"Callie." Mason said gently. He waited. Callie had to look at him. He was looking at her very sympathetically. "I am asking you to let me help you. If you don't want my help that's fine, but at least acknowledge that you don't have to do everything all the time and that it is okay to let others take your burden sometimes."

Callie was shocked. Somehow she hadn't considered that her friends might want to help. She just thought that they would feel like she was being demanding.

"Oh! Um, it's just, well, I guess I didn't want you to think I was acting helpless to get stuff, or…something."

"We know that you are an extraordinarily capable and beautiful woman. None of us can do everything. Maybe that's why we make friends to start with, so that none of us has to pretend to be super men or women." He again held out his hand to her. "May I help you?"

"Yes, thank you." Callie said shyly as she put her hand on Mason's arm and he began to help her down the aisle of the jet.

"And was that so very hard?"

"Sort of."

Mason laughed. "I think you will be just fine."

"Is it really okay if I am at your house?"

"Of course. I have several extra rooms, and an extra bathroom. I don't have to be around you if you don't want. No one does. We just want you to be safe, for a while. Besides, if you have trouble sleeping or from PTSD, I would rather be where I can do the most good soon as possible. That means being in the same building."

"Okay. Is James going to be there?"

"Well, Callie, that is really up to you."

Callie thought about it for a few minutes as they made it out of the plane and began to walk to a car. "I think I would like him to be in the same house, at least. I am afraid to let him be somewhere else."

"That is understandable. It will be no problem, I promise."

"Are you sure?"

"Even if it were a problem, I would lie about it." Mason said calmly.

"Mason!"

"Look at it this way; you won't know either way. Just take my word that it is no problem."

"But..."

"I was joking. Believe me, I need my friends. I wouldn't start lying this fucking late in the game; it would ruin far more than the temporary gain of the lie."

"That was mean!" She accused.

Mason shrugged. "Why?"

"What?"

"Why was it mean?"

"Because..." Callie was surprised again. What did Mason even mean? There was no 'why'; it was just mean, wasn't it? "Because you make it seem like it doesn't matter what I think just because the end is the same."

"Exactly. The ends do not justify the means to get there. The means matter, deeply. That's what I wanted you to think about. And yes, it was fucking mean. It was mean to suggest that you are not intelligent enough to make your own decisions and come to your own conclusions. It was mean to say that you don't matter, that the only thing that matters is how I want you to think."

"Yes, all that!"

Mason smiled again. "And that is why you matter, my dear. You matter because you are infinitely more important that any fucking pathetic attempts to manipulate you. Remember that."

"Is this how you normally do therapy?"

"No, usually I am way more professional, and usually my clients aren't nearly as charming or good-looking." They had made it to the car and Mason opened the door for her.

Callie smiled. "You are so much like Porter sometimes."

"I know. Or perhaps, he is like me. If you want my opinion, I think we have grown more like each other. That happens with people who love each other, I have noticed. He's my best friend. It'd be strange if we didn't influence each other somehow."

James was standing by the car, looking a bit apprehensive. Callie remembered that she was supposed to tell him if he could be in the house with her. It seemed important that she make it his choice. "James, I would like for you to come to Mason's house with me, if that is all right with you. I promise to not be upset if you would rather be somewhere else."

James smiled. "Where else would I want to be? I was only waiting to see if that was what you needed." He got in the back seat and Callie slid into the other side.

"All right, children," Mason said as he started the car and began driving. "My name is Mason and I will be your driver today. First and last stop is my house and then you two may do whatever the hell it is you two do."

"Eat. Sleep. Shower. Repeat." James said.

"Very good." Mason signaled for a turn at a red light. "I have two guest rooms. You two figure it all out."

"I'll take one and Callie can have the other." James shrugged.

Callie nodded. "Agreed. I'm still tired."

Mason glanced back. "You will be for quite a while, I think. It takes a long time to recover from that sort of trauma."

"Damn."

"Sorry."

Chapter 31

Callie saw little of Mason over the next two days. James and Porter returned to the store together with Michael along. Juan was off doing whatever he did, something with computers, and Callie stayed at Mason's house. She knew Sienna was right next door and that she could call if she needed something. Other than that, she lounged and did very little and loved every minute of it.

The evening of the second day, James came in looking very pleased. Callie suspected it had something to do with work, but she couldn't get him to tell her anything. Even pouting outrageously didn't do anything.

Porter and Sienna invited them to play cards, so Callie and James went there for dinner. It was very laid-back and fun, although Callie drank a little too much. It might have been the alcohol, which was high proof or it might have been something else. Whatever happened, Callie was a little tipsy.

"Ah, I had better go. I am going to get sick if I don't." She said, throwing her hand in. "I drank too much already."

Porter sighed theatrically. "Oh, fine. You had better walk her home, James. We don't want her to get in trouble in her shit-faced condition."

James laughed. "That would be tragic, for sure."

"I'm not shit-faced!" Callie protested hotly.

Porter raised an eyebrow. "Oh, really?"

"No!"

"Whatever. We'll see you later, you two."

Back at Mason's house, James turned to go from the room Callie was staying in. She grabbed his sleeve impulsively. "Stay."

James looked uncertain. "Callie, you're drunk. I don't want something to happen because we're both tipsy."

"I'm not that drunk, James. I want you to stay with me. I promise I'll be good."

"Why do I not believe you?"

"I don't know. I am so amazingly believable."

James laughed. "You are tipsy, aren't you?"

"Yes. Now get over here, please."

James smiled at her. "All right. What do you want to do?"

"Kiss me first and let's see what else happens after that."

It was significantly later. Callie and James had both fallen asleep after some extended kissing, although nothing more had happened. There was a knock on the door. Callie woke up, initially confused. The knock came again. She sighed and got up, trying to not wake James. Absently she straightened her shirt as she opened the door. Mason was in the hall, looking distracted.

"Oh, Mason! I didn't expect to see you." Callie said as she came out and closed the door softly.

"Who the hell did you think it would be, Callie?"

"Um, I don't know. That didn't sound very smart, did it?"

Mason shrugged. "I was more curious who you thought it would be. Do you know where James is?"

Callie gestured over her shoulder. "In there sleeping. We went to Porter and Sienna's."

Mason nodded. He still seemed very distracted. "Good. I need to talk to him, but later. I need to talk to you now."

"Okay." Callie's natural curiosity grew stronger; Mason was rarely this serious. Whatever it was, it had to be important. She followed him to his study. His black cat Ninja slipped in and jumped on the desk. Absently, Mason petted him.

"Sit, Callie. This might take a while. Would you like anything to drink?"

"Water, please."

Mason poured a glass. "I've asked Porter to come over when he is dressed. We can wait until he gets here."

"Porter was awake at this hour?"

Mason smiled slightly. "Porter wakes up a lot. He responded to a text I sent earlier. He's awake."

"Where have you been, anyway? I haven't seen you."

"That's part of what we have to discuss, actually. I've been doing specialized research."

Porter entered softly. Callie watched him move. Although his lightness wasn't as surprising as Michael's it was much the same. Porter saw her watching him and raised an eyebrow. "Is there something?"

Callie looked away quickly. "Um, no, not really."

"Fucking bullshit."

"Well, it's just that you move a lot like Michael. That's all. I didn't really notice before."

"That stands to reason, since I used to be a fairly decent boxer."

"You were?"

"That was a long time ago, but yes. What the hell brought this on, anyway?"

"I just noticed it. That's how I knew it was Michael in the cell. I recognized how he moves."

Porter smiled suddenly. "You are quite amazing."

Callie wasn't sure what that meant. She blushed a little. "Are you making fun of me?"

"No, I am quite serious. Not many people would make that realization and recognize someone based on it, and fewer would connect the way he moves as a trained fighter and someone who is ready to fight. That takes a remarkable person."

Mason nodded. "Which is why I asked you both here. This next step might depend on you, Callie."

"Oh. Damn."

"Precisely. Porter, take a seat. I need your help. Do you want something to drink?"

"I already had my fucking allotment."

"I'll fucking bend the rules for you."

"Then yes. One scotch on the rocks."

"Pour it yourself." Mason gestured to the sideboard. "I hope I didn't wake you up with the text."

"No, I was awake anyway."

"Oh?" Porter's face reddened slightly. Mason nodded. "I see. Well, I am glad you could make it over afterward."

Porter laughed. "She's sleeping now. I told her where I would be and she told me to fucking leave and let her sleep."

"Good. At least you won't be wanting to hurry back."

"No, I have done what I needed to do tonight."

Mason smiled slightly. "The reason I need you both here is because I have been trying to make a connection with that hit on Mahmoud's office and your being there. As far as I can tell, no one knew the ladies would be there, correct, Porter?"

Porter shrugged. "I don't think James and I mentioned it to anybody really, since it is none of their damn business."

"Exactly. And Emil was surprised to find them there. It was like he seized an opportunity."

"Seemed like it."

"That hit was risky. It wasn't in character, and Mahmoud wasn't a big player in the diamond world. Why did they hit him specifically?"

"You've said all this before, Mason."

"Boo the fuck hoo. It helps me think to lay it out. I still need the fucking trigger. Hence you are here instead of in your nice bed with your beautiful wife. The sooner you help, the sooner you can go home."

"Fine, whatever, bitch. Start laying it out then."

"I think it was one of the diamond cabal."

Porter sat up very straight. "What the fuck!"

"There was a lot of communication happening between John the Gent and Emil. It picked up very significantly last year after your last big run. When you launched the Celtic Dream line, all of sudden John the Gent was talking with Emil all the fucking time."

"Bastard! I will fucking beat the shit out of him!"

"Like hell you will. You fucking get a handle on yourself."

Porter snorted but subsided.

"Which one is John the Gent?" Callie asked.

"Jonathon Tyler."

"Oh! I know that name."

"His nickname is John the Gent." Porter said as he stood up to get another drink. "He gave it to himself because he never acts like a gentleman."

"Oh. So what about him?"

Mason sighed. "Here's the way this has to work, you two. James can't go in. John doesn't like men. He only deals with them. He dotes on beautiful women, though. Also he wants to have a reputation as a ladies' man. Callie, you have to do it. Sienna is out; he knows who she is by sight. Because James is still technically Porter's assistant, he isn't well-known yet, and therefore neither are you."

"That is fucking bullshit." Porter said shortly. "He's a fucking partner."

Mason glared at Porter. "Porter, honestly, do we have to fucking argue the damn semantics right the fuck now? It's fucking one-thirty in the morning!"

"It's fucking shit!"

"I don't fucking care! It's how the world fucking works!"

"Yeah, fine, whatever."

Mason shook his head distractedly. "Fucking hell, Porter. You drive me fucking insane sometimes."

"It's fucking good for you."

"Whatever. Anyway, I will have Juan make something that we can bug you with, Callie. You will have to act aloof but interested, like those rich bitches you knew at school."

Callie giggled. "Okay. I know exactly what you mean."

"Also, you can't show that you know anything when he starts spilling it. Porter, you have to train her, and train her fast. We have to move on this shit before the real news gets out. It has to be a few days at most."

"Okay, Mason. I can do that."

"One more thing: Porter, do you have a fantastic diamond? You know what I mean. It has to grab his attention and hold it."

"I think I do. I have a rare icy blue two carat beauty in a unique cut. I bought it from a little-known man; it should be the right thing. I need to custom set it though. Right now it is loose." He paused, squinting at Callie. "I think a white gold necklace. What do you think, Mason?"

Mason nodded. "Whatever, man. You are the expert. Juan might need to incorporate the bug into a piece of jewelry. Do you have anything that might work?"

"Bracelet. I have one that is missing a setting. It can be built right in and no one will know."

"Good. Then you two are on the job."

Porter looked at Callie again. "Are you sleepy?"

"No, not really. Not anymore."

"Then let's play some poker. We need to work on hiding your tells first." Callie gave a huge sigh. Porter laughed. "It's the best way I know to get it down. Shall we?"

Chapter 32

They had moved back to Mason's kitchen. Porter had a big pitcher of water and some glasses off to the side and a pile of chips in front of him. "The first thing I need you to do is assume your character. You are no longer Callie. Now you are Seraphim, nickname Sera. In case you are unaware, that is the name of one of the classes of angels. Therefore, you are to pretend you are so fucking far above everybody you think you are an actual angel. Assume it now." Porter poured two glasses of water and looked at Mason. "You hanging around, Mason? Do you want to be dealt in?"

"No. I have some shit to get arranged. I will check in around two. You shouldn't push too hard tonight, Porter. She might need time."

Porter shrugged. "I'll try to be nice."

Mason snorted. "Whatever, bitch."

"I might. You can never fucking tell."

Mason went back towards his study. Porter looked back at Callie. "Your character. Assume it now as fully as you can. You must be Sera in all ways, including how you think of yourself. That's the key. You must be Sera. Callie does not exist. The name is the place to hang the character. You are Seraphim. Who is she? What does she think like? What does she, or you, do? How do you react, as Seraphim? How do you speak? How do you dress? You must decide all that and assume it all."

Callie took a drink and tried to think herself into the character of Seraphim. This was going to be a struggle. Porter was watching her closely. He nodded once. "Okay, I am going to deal. I want you to be Seraphim. Answer only to that name, if you can. Act as fully as you can. Try to assume different speech patterns, different habits, all of it. Let's play."

Callie looked at her cards. "Stop." Porter said and she looked up, a little concerned that she'd done something wrong already. "No, Sera, you have to be in control of the situation. Don't look startled. Look annoyed. Who is this cheap shit that is correcting you? That's who you are. Let's keep going."

Callie nodded at her cards, acting like she didn't care at all what Porter said. She tried to pretend she hasn't even heard. Who dealt this shit anyway? Porter laughed softly. "That's it, Sera, perfect. Keep that up."

Callie counted her chips idly to hide the surge of triumph she felt. She wanted Porter to approve. She threw in two with as much disdain as she could manage. "Open."

"Call." Porter also threw in two. "And bump." He added one.

Callie stared at him for a few moments. How dare he? "Call." She tossed in one more.

Porter lay his hand down. "Two pair, queen high."

Callie tossed her hand disgustedly. "Whatever. Take it." She looked at the wall as he pulled the pot towards his side.

"Ante up, Sera, if you want in this hand." Porter said as he shuffled again.

The game proceeded with Porter offering advice or critiques at different moments. Callie couldn't tell if he was pleased with her performance or not; he acted just like he was playing cards with a real person named Seraphim. Towards the end, when she got tired, Callie caught herself actually thinking she was Sera. That revelation caused her to jerk upright and she inadvertently knocked her chips off the table.

"Oh, I am so sorry!" Callie started to clean up.

Porter grinned at her, his eyes twinkling outrageously. "It's a bit of a wake-up, isn't it?"

"Oh my gosh, yes!"

"Just keep a leash on which you really are, Callie. You've done very well tonight. I think a little more coaching and you will be ready." Callie glowed. She wanted to impress Porter. If he asked, she would deny it, but to herself she was honest enough to admit that his approval meant a great deal.

There was the sound of soft clapping form the kitchen area. Mason was applauding gravely.

"How long have you been there?" Callie asked, a bit

embarrassed. She hadn't expected to be watched.

"Long enough. You have done quite well. And don't be too worried. We'll be there to end it all with you. You won't have to hold it all alone."

"Thank goodness."

Porter nodded. "She should be ready by tomorrow afternoon. John the Gent doesn't do anything before three, and hopefully that gives me enough time to set that damn stone."

"You don't have any choice, Porter. It must be done by then."

"I know, and that somehow fails to comfort me."

"Whatever, go home and fucking sleep it off."

Porter bowed mockingly and left. Mason helped Callie restack the chips. "You really have done well, Callie. It isn't the easiest thing to do and you have managed it convincingly. You aren't trying to be someone who already exists; you are making up Sera from your own mind. Go to sleep, beautiful lady. Let it all pass into dreams for a while." Callie felt another surge of satisfaction.

"Okay, Mason. I just hope it works."

Mason raised an eyebrow at her. "It has to work, Callie. There is no other choice."

"Amazingly, that doesn't make me feel any better. Just like Porter said."

Mason shrugged impudently. "I'll give you the same answer then: go and fucking sleep it off."

"You are impossible." Callie laughed.

"I know. I learned it from the master himself."

"Which, Juan or Porter or Michael?"

"Any. All. Go to sleep."

Callie smiled as she walked back to her room. This might even be a little fun. She was anxious but the sense of adventure was starting to force that anxiety aside. She wanted to prove to herself that she was smarter and better than this John jerk. With the coaching Porter had given her and the reassurance that she wouldn't be alone, she felt that she was more than capable. It was a new feeling for Callie and she didn't want to lose it.

Chapter 33

Although she didn't have a time she needed to be up, Callie found she couldn't sleep past six-thirty. She was just too excited. Quietly she got up, being careful to not wake James.

She showered quickly and got some new clothes. Mason had somehow managed to find some nice things for her.

Mason and Porter were in the kitchen area talking quietly. Porter looked over as she entered and suddenly his eyes twinkled. "Good morning, Sera. How are you this morning?"

Immediately, Callie raised her head and stared at him with great disdain. She didn't even realize what she was doing until Porter grinned. "You are so fucking ready for this. Did you see how she just became Seraphim, Mason? Wasn't that fucking perfect?"

Mason nodded. "Yes, now quit congratulating yourself." Porter laughed. Mason smiled slightly at Callie. "Very good, indeed, Callie. I know it seemed a bit much last night but you are ready. I would not like to be John today."

"John the Jerk?" Callie asked, accepting a cup of coffee from Mason.

Porter laughed uproariously. "You better not call him that to his face!"

"Oh, oops." Callie smiled. She sipped at her coffee as Mason cut some fruit up.

Porter, still smiling, stood up. "I have to get that setting done. Juan is coming with me and he is going to wire the bracelet for you. We should be back by one."

"Good." Mason said ungraciously. "Bring some clothes with you for this Seraphim person."

"Will do, Mason. Callie." Porter bowed extravagantly and left.

"He's the best, isn't he?" Callie asked Mason.

"Of course. That's why he gets away with what he does. What would you like for breakfast?"

After a half hour, James came to breakfast and Sienna also came over. Mason and James went back to Mason's study to have some discussion, leaving Callie and Sienna together in the living room.

"So, Callie, Porter tells me that you have created a truly wonderful character between the two of you." Sienna said, smiling.

"Would you like to meet her?"

Sienna laughed. "No, I don't think so. Rich bitches set my teeth on edge, for some reason."

"Me, too. They always expect me to pander to them, or something."

"Maybe that's it. I often get the idea that they think I am trying to show off, as if I think I am not good enough so I am compensating with my looks."

"Well, Sienna, that's probably what everyone thinks, to be honest."

"I know, but it gets old quick. Since when are beautiful women precluded from being intelligent? You know what I mean."

"I don't, not really."

Sienna smiled at Callie. "Oh, really? I don't believe you. You may not realize it, though. Why do you think those rich acquaintances of yours made you feel so inferior? It is my experience that they are jealous, really fucking jealous."

"You're joking."

"No, I'm not. You are quite beautiful and the way that many women show jealousy is in trying to make the beautiful one feel insecure. It is like a trade-off."

Callie wasn't sure how to answer that. She took a sip of her tea and Sienna didn't mention it again.

James and Mason returned after a while.

"Are you going out?" Callie asked James.

"No, I will be wherever you are, along with Mason, Porter, and Michael. We promised to protect you."

"Oh, that's right. I sort of forgot."

Mason sat in the recliner. "Michael is going to be your driver. No

206

one of that status would be without some sort of help. That way, he can be close by. Juan will monitor the bug from here and he will relay everything to us. Of course, we should be able to blend in to the background, too."

"Where are we going to be?"

"Oh, did I forget to mention that? Really?"

Sienna nodded, smiling. "Yes, Mason. You seem to be losing your memory as you get old."

Mason sighed. "It happens to the best of us."

"What, you get fucking senile?"

"No, we get fucking old. Now, Callie, you and Michael are going to be at The Strawberry Patch. I will be one of the wait staff. I already have that arranged. Porter is just going to have to suck it up wherever he can. Sera will be there, John the idiot will show up whenever he does. He has frequented it for several weeks now, but I am not only banking on that. I have left a tantalizingly vague hint for him that a rich, beautiful, single young lady might have asked about him. Since he thinks I am working there, well, you can see that he will fucking take the bait."

"May he fucking choke on it." Sienna said gravely.

"Amen." James nodded.

Mason sat back comfortably. "Now we just wait until Porter and Johnny boy get here. We can't do shit till they do, except I have to be at work at two. Let's find something else to talk about."

Around twelve-thirty, as they were having a leisurely lunch, Mason, who had been in the kitchen getting drinks, came out with a triumphant smile. "They are on their way now. We can have this all hammered out by the time I have to leave."

Porter and Juan came in soon afterwards, each carrying a small wrapped box.

Juan was his usual self. "Hey, Mason, got anything to eat? You sent me with a damn slave driver and I haven't even had time for lunch yet."

"You could have fucking got yourself something." Porter retorted.

207

"Shut up, Porter. You said we had to get the damn thing done."

Mason gravely handed Juan a plate of food. "Yes! Awesome! Good shit!" Juan said enthusiastically, setting the box on the table.

Porter snorted. "Any more?" He asked Mason, also setting his box down. Mason smiled slightly and handed him another plate.

As Porter and Juan ate, Callie fidgeted. She was starting to feel anxious about the plan again. At one point, Porter glanced at her and winked roguishly.

"He likes this sort of thing, doesn't he?" Callie whispered to Sienna.

She smiled. "Of course. He likes outsmarting people. And he likes being an insufferable ass about it all."

Callie laughed. Porter smiled. "I heard that, Sienna."

"Oh, damn, I am soooo sorry." She said sarcastically.

"Do tell." He returned with heavy emphasis.

"Fucking serves you right. Don't listen in on conversations that aren't yours and you won't hear things that upset you."

"But then I won't know things. I can't stand not knowing things."

Sienna raised her eyebrow and said nothing. Porter's eyes twinkled. Callie shook her head. "You are both just too much."

"Agreed." Mason said, cutting the conversation off. "I have to get going, so let's get the shit laid out and all. What do you have, Johnny?"

Juan shoved his box at Mason. Mason carefully unwrapped the string holding the lid on. He took out a gold filigree bangle with discreet jewels tucked into it. "That white one, there by the hinge, that's the bug."

Mason examined it carefully. "I can't even tell. Good job, you two. If we can't spot it, no way a casual glance will, even by an expert. What do you think, James?" He passed it over.

James looked closely. "Without a loupe, this is impossible to tell."

"Good." Mason handed it to Callie and she slipped it on.

"Now, there is a location indicator and an audible transmitter." Juan said. "It was all I could pack in there. If you wanted visual, it would have to be more obvious."

"No, this is perfect." Mason said. "We'll be there, anyway. The visual will be a given."

"That's what I figured. I will monitor the signals and pass you info on these." He handed Mason and Porter a very small ear device. "You should be able to hear me, but you won't be able to talk to me. You have cell phones for that. And there's one for Mikey, just in case something happens."

Mason nodded. "And Porter, your show-stopper?"

Porter smiled and pushed his box across to Mason. Instead of opening it, Mason passed it to Callie. "This is for you, I believe."

Callie opened the box and held up the diamond. It seemed suspended in a web of wire. "Oh, Porter! This is amazing!"

James smiled. "Hand it over. I want to see what a rushed piece looks like from him!"

Porter laughed. "That's not fucking fair!"

"Oh? Too bad." James looked it over carefully. "Yes, I like the feeling of it. It is obvious that you did not spend your usual time."

"It's not supposed to look like mine."

James shrugged and handed it back to Callie. "It doesn't. It is almost generic. Perfect job."

"Generic?" Mason smiled. "I rather think not."

"I meant that it has no personal characteristics like most jewelers try to put in."

"That's better." Mason looked at his watch and stood up. "Michael will be here by two. I have to get going. Callie, or should I say Sera, I shall see you later."

Chapter 34

By three, Callie was in the Strawberry Patch. It was discreetly decorated with obviously expensive items. The chandeliers were giving forth muted light. A string quartet played softly in the background. Callie thought the place almost reeked of obsequiousness.

She sat at a table off to the side, a journal open and a newspaper on the other side. She occasionally wrote things in the journal. She wore gloves and expensively understated clothes. The fantastic diamond was on, radiating its beauty. Michael had softly been to another room, and when he came back, he slipped into a seat beside her.

"You can see that fucking thing all the way across the damn room." He murmured.

"Good. I would hate to be overlooked."

"No problem there."

"Can you see the bruises?"

"No, not until you are close up.

"Good."

"He should be here soon. Become Seraphim."

Callie nodded once and assumed an icy indifference.

Michael gave no indication that she had changed. He was obviously scanning the room and ready. Callie had noticed Mason passing through once, his entire body the picture of servile help. Damn but they were good at this.

After a while, she scanned the room idly. There were several groups of people, some obviously business men on their breaks, some couples who might or might not have been married. She didn't see John the Gent yet. He'd better get down here soon.

A slight stir at the entrance caught her attention. A group of men came in and stood surveying the room. Michael exhaled slightly. It must be him. No one else would cause Michael to go to another state of awareness like that. Feigning no interest, Callie turned a page in her journal and began to write her impression of an article about a conflict somewhere. She made certain to not look up. Seraphim would not look

210

up.

Presently, there came a soft step. "Excuse me, madam." A soft voice said. Callie looked up briskly. Mason stood there, his face as blank as if he had never seen her before. He held a small tray with a folded paper on it. "A gentleman asked me to give this to you."

Callie took the paper and gestured sharply. Mason bowed and moved off. It was a heavy paper. She glanced at it. The monogram at the top was for Jonathon Tyler. Below that, there were the words, "May I have the compliment of meeting you?"

Callie kept a smile from her face. She took a sheet from her journal, wrote a short assent and handed it to Michael. "Take this to the gentleman." She said without looking at Michael and returning to her journal. Michael was gone and back with hardly a sound. Callie ignored him.

"Excuse me, lady." A smooth, unctuous voice said softly. Callie looked up and recognized John the Gent. He bowed and she extended a gloved hand to him, which he took carefully.

"Would you care to sit?" Callie asked distantly, gesturing to one of the chairs at the table. John hesitated, looking carefully at Michael. "My manservant." Callie dismissed the implied question. "I go nowhere without him."

"Ah. He is formidable."

"One of the reasons I have him." When this was over, she was going to have to apologize to Michael for treating him like he was nothing.

It was evidently how John the Gent expected her to react though. He smiled and sat. "Lady, you have a truly remarkable diamond." He ventured.

"Yes. I have been told so. I chose it specifically for the quality of the stone."

"And the setting is quite unique. You are quite complimentary to it."

"I prefer to think of the setting being something which compliments me, not the other way around." Callie said coldly.

211

"Of course. And what is your name, if I might be so bold as to ask?"

Callie stared at him for a few seconds. "Seraphim. However, those close to me call me Sera."

"Seraphim. Truly a beautiful name for a beautiful woman."

Callie inclined her head. "And you are?"

"My name is Jonathon Tyler. I work in diamonds, so you may understand my interest in your necklace."

Callie nodded, still distant. She waited. He would make his move fairly soon. He had to. The social convention was to either move on her or move off.

"May I join you for a drink, Seraphim?" He asked, perhaps a touch quickly, but she wasn't going to hold it against him. She was supposed to be aloof, not rude.

"I think that would be very nice." Callie raised her hand carelessly. The black-coated waiter who appeared was silent and efficient. "I would like another jasmine tea. Bring this gentleman what he wishes." As a rule, restaurants like this never asked who would pay. John ordered a brandy.

They chatted for a while over surface matters. Callie could tell he wanted to know more about her necklace, but it would have been rude to ask outright.

After about an hour of polite conversation, John rose and extended a hand to Callie. "Would you care to join me in a private booth?"

Callie pretended to consider. "All right, but I must insist that my servant be allowed to stand outside. He is most protective of my person." Well, that was no lie; Michael had threatened to rip the arms off the guy already.

John smiled indulgently. "But of course!" He nodded graciously to Michael. Callie laid several bills on the table and handed her journal and newspaper to Michael and laid her hand on John's arm. She pretended to not notice as he winked outrageously to the group he had come in with. Let them think they'd pulled one over another rich naïve woman. She could afford to wait.

Once they were in the private booth, Callie stirred her tea idly. "You mentioned you were in diamonds." She said carefully. "What do you do? I have interests in that market."

John took a long drink of whatever he had. "I buy and sell, mainly. I am a mediator for several groups. I have several extensive contacts in Africa and Asia for that purpose."

"Oh?" Callie raised her eye brows appreciatively and looked back into her tea glass. "That sounds most promising, Mr. Tyler."

He warmed to the implication that she might be willing to invest in him. "Yes, I have had some recent discussions with my factors in Asia..." He continued to discuss his business dealings in China for the next few minutes. Callie expressed reserved interest. China didn't interest her much. She wanted him to focus back on Africa.

'Where did you buy your own diamond, Miss...?"

"You may call me Sera. My friends do." Callie smiled slightly. She couldn't give him anything that could be checked out, including a last name. "I bought the stone at market."

"Ah." That seemed to not interest him much. Diamond markets were quite anonymous. "Was it cut?"

"Yes, I bought it loose and it was set here."

"Oh? The setting is quite stunning as well. Who set it for you?" John's eyes were quite shrewd and seemed to Callie to be too interested. She'd have to skate that question.

She shrugged. "I do not know."

"Really?" Now he sounded very skeptical. Clearly he thought she would have to remember who made such a special piece.

"Of course not." Callie said coldly. "I instructed my private secretary to see to it for me. I do not handle such chores myself." She purposely looked back at her drink, dismissing the very idea.

"Oh, of course." He still sounded skeptical, but much less so.

Callie didn't even bother to explain further. He could believe her or not, but she was not going to sound pathetic by adding more lies on. Porter and Mason had taught her that before: never bog down a perfectly good lie with more details than needed. She merely sipped at her tea.

There was a bit of silence while he regrouped and she thought of how to lead him back to his contacts. She set down her drink and said carelessly, "Do you do much business in rough stone?"

"Sometimes. I mostly try to buy cut stones."

"That is unfortunate for me. I have a few interests in patronizing some up and coming names. They are mostly in the cutting and faceting business, and I have been thinking of leveraging certain resources to make rough stone more available to them. That would require some significant quality stone, however."

"Yes, it would, indeed. I do have some contacts in Africa."

"Ah? I have interests in the city of Tangier already in place. It would be more useful to me to use existing shipping interests." That was risky. She knew it, but she also couldn't think of another city right off-hand. Tangier was a big shipping hub.

John stirred his own drink thoughtfully. "There aren't many diamond sellers in Tangier."

"Ah, well, it would have been the best for me."

"There are other ways to get the diamonds to your shipping networks. For example, we might be able to buy in Bou Arle; I have contacts there. And I have contact with several people who operate outside the established sellers."

"Oh? You do? That interests me more. I find that those who work on their own are more reliable than those who do not. And frankly, I don't much care how they get the diamonds, so long as the quality is good and the stones are significant size."

John smiled. "I have several who might be interested in supplying you then."

"Very good. Do any of them come to Tangier?"

"They might, for a price."

"That is of no concern to me at this time. "

214

"I can think of at least one man who has been willing to go into Tangier for a special purchase."

"Excellent. Does he deliver the proper goods?"

John chuckled indulgently. "He certainly does. He went above and beyond for me and my partner."

"Your partner?"

"Yes. Since you are in the market, you may have heard of him. Senator Ford?"

"Oh, yes, the oil magnate. But I did not realize he was in the diamond business too."

"He isn't. At least, not on the surface." John winked and Callie took it to mean that the senator was the money behind some of the enterprises. "He wanted that special package although he didn't say why. I have since learned that he had personal reasons for the pickup."

"Ah." Callie feigned polite interest, but it was getting hard to keep her emotions in check.

John obviously wanted to impress her with his contacts and his double-dealing on them, because he kept right on talking. "I learned from his secretary that the senator had suspicions about one of the operatives. Maybe he thought he was not getting what he ordered."

"Very possibly." Callie agreed and took a sip from her tea. "But your own contact; he provided what the senator wanted, then?"

"Absolutely."

"If I may be so indiscreet, did he ask for stones?"

"Among other services. The stones were of the quality that was expected."

"I wonder how much his services cost. I might need to contact someone with that sort of business sense." Callie suggested.

"You can't contact him. He only listens to me." John bragged, taking a large drink. "I can get a hold of him next week, if you have the capital and if you have some specific instructions."

"I have the capital, but I need the details of the services he can provide. I refuse to put up money without any idea of what I am getting

215

in return."

John looked a bit unsettled. Callie let him think on it for a little bit. She wouldn't push this just yet, but she needed more to catch them both.

"If you are interested in another…partner… you can see the quality of the men I patronize." Callie said presently, gesturing to her necklace. "I may not know them all by sight, but I guarantee the goods."

"Yes. That is true. It is unique and expertly done." John mused. He toyed with his cell phone absently. "It is quite a tempting offer."

Callie shrugged. "I might be willing to offer more than a standard partnership, should I think the terms right."

John grinned. "That's an offer, for sure."

Callie smiled back. "I find it helps to know what all the terms are beforehand."

"That's quite a bargaining chip you hold, Sera."

"I know."

Chapter 35

John the Gent was considering it. He drank his scotch distractedly. Callie let him think in silence. The next move was his and she would have to respond then. It would do no good to plan something now and have it upset.

"Well, let's look at what you might want done by my factors."

Callie smiled. "Let's look at what your factors have already done or are willing to do." She countered. "I don't try to do business without knowing the exact jobs to ask of people."

"I have some small-scale smuggling in place, and some of the factors have arranged hits."

"What kind of hit? I don't want to be involved in anything that might spiral into a vendetta. That would be unacceptable. Nothing must be traced to my person or my business."

"No, nothing that big. There have been some small robberies here and there in places. Take that Tangier one. It was a small specialized robbery with some casualties."

"Casualties? That smacks of juvenility. I cannot condone sloppy work. I insist on utmost professionalism and killing because of a mistake is not something I accept."

John smirked. "No, my dear, you misunderstand: the casualties were part of the package deal. I have it in confidence that Senator Ford wished to even a score with a certain craftsman who had snubbed him repeatedly. He wanted to send a strong message to other craftsmen that he is not to be denied."

"I see." Callie nodded, looking back at her glass and stirring it again. She was having trouble keeping this up. She wanted to end the charade and get away from him as soon as she could.

The privacy curtain twitched slightly. Mason came in with his servile manner. "Sir, a pardon, but there is a note from a gentleman for you."

John, obviously not pleased to be interrupted, held out his hand impatiently. "Very well. Let me have it."

217

"Of course, sir." Mason handed a small folded note to him.

John opened and glanced at it. "What does this mean? All it says is 'Got you.'"

"It means," said Porter, stepping through the curtain, "That you are seriously fucked."

"What? How are you here?" John stood up quickly. He obviously didn't take surprise as well as he might have thought he did. The drink he held sloshed about the glass and onto the tablecloth. He didn't seem to notice as he gaped incredulously at Porter.

"The same way I am." James said quietly, also coming through the curtain.

John seemed to be beyond responding. He merely stared with his mouth open.

"Also, I would suggest that you not be quite so eager to brag about your exploits next time, if there ever is a next time."

Callie stood to leave. John looked at her, his eyes narrowing. "Who are you, really? I want the truth." He asked dangerously.

"Truth, my dear sir? As that famous man in history said, 'What is truth?' Oh, I admit I might have lied a time or two. My name won't mean anything to you, not really, but I do have a special message for you." Callie said calmly.

"And what is that?"

Callie punched him across the face. It probably would have worked better if she had known what she was doing, but she didn't care. It felt amazing. "Don't fucking stick you face where it doesn't belong again. I am quite sure the message will be passed along to Senator Ford, as well. Good day, Mr. Tyler."

Porter smiled and bowed to her as he held the curtain open. Michael was just outside. He escorted her quickly out of the restaurant.

"What happened to your arm?" He asked softly. "You're holding it funny."

"I punched him in the face. Would you mind giving me some lessons sometime? I think I did it wrong."

Michael laughed. "There is no wrong way, so long as you only have to do it once. But yes, you should have some lessons. That's pretty fucking important in this line of work, and you definitely deserve to be among the best in the field." He held the car door open. "Shall we?"

"We shall."

As they drove off, Michael glanced in his mirror a couple times. Callie noticed that she didn't know where they were going.

"Michael, where are we going? This isn't the way back to Mason's house, is it?" She asked, curious again.

"No, it's not. There's a tail back there, and I am going to either fucking lose him or else I am going to lead him somewhere and fucking put him in traction."

"Oh. Um, if it comes to that, would you mind not doing it where I can see?"

"No problem. I don't think it will go there though. I usually can lose a tail." He made right turn. "I haven't had a fight I haven't planned on in a long time."

"Oh. Good." Callie's wrist was starting to hurt. "This hurts. Can I do something for it?"

Michael made a left and parked. He turned in the seat. "Let me see." He bent it back and forwards a time or two. "It will probably swell a bit but you should be all right. Let me bandage it a little to keep it still and we can get Mason to look at it later."

"How much later?"

Michael winked. "A hell of a lot later, I think. You got a huge bombshell out of that idiot. Perfect job."

Callie blushed. "Thank you."

"Mason will have to sort it out with Washington."

"Have you ever been there?"

Michael shrugged. "Once or twice. The last time I punched a hole in the wall of the Secretary of Homeland Security's office."

"Michael!"

"He deserved it. Acting like a fucking teenager. Pissed me off."

He eased back into traffic.

Callie shook her head. "You are amazing sometimes."

"Mason chewed my ass for it later. Whatever, it worked. I don't fucking do bullies like that."

Callie smiled. "I can imagine it was quite convincing!"

Michael nodded. "Either it was or Porter offering to trash his office was. We had a bit of fun with it all. Let's cruise the main drag. I bet I can shake his ass after three blocks."

"What do you want to bet?" Callie countered.

"You've been hanging out with Juan and Porter too much. I bet you a beer of the choosing of the winner."

"You've got yourself a bet."

"I am warning you that I am going to ask for the most fucking expensive beer I can find."

"Yes, I know. Also, I wanted to apologize for pretending to treat you like dirt back there."

"I know you didn't mean it."

"No, but even faking it isn't acceptable."

"I understand. I forgive you. Fair enough?"

"Thank you, Michael."

"You're welcome, Callie. Let me lose this idiot back there and then we can get back to safety and relax."

"Relax?"

"I know how it can be hard to hold a fake person up; you need to be yourself and let that fake person wash off."

"You're right. Let us go, then!"

Epilogue

Mason watched the officers take the senator out of the office in the Capitol building from a side hall. He smiled in satisfaction. All because of one pretty woman they had this guy's ass.

"Thank you, Doctor Briggs." The Secretary said quietly from behind him. "We might not have had enough to pin him without you and your team."

"You're welcome, sir." Mason said just as quietly. "If you will excuse me, I have a small party to attend."

The small party was of course with his friends. They were gathering at Juan's house this time. Mason was going to be a little late, but there was nothing to do about that. He couldn't make the plane fly any faster than it was.

By the time he arrived, it was obvious that the usual suspects were all there. Rather than knock, he opened the front door and walked in.

"Mason!" Gabriella greeted him. "Thank you for getting here as soon as you could."

"It is my pleasure, Gabriella. I had a little problem to take care of, but now that he's all tied up, I am free for a while. Pour me a drink; I haven't had anything for several hours."

"But of course!" She laughed. "To the kitchen we go. Everyone else is in the study playing cards, of course."

"I am glad they didn't wait on me."

"I had to do some serious persuading of Michael and Juan on that point, but they came around."

The study was informal and fun. The game was quite loud, and that was exactly what Mason needed. "Deal me in, you old pirate." He ordered Porter as he sat down.

"Of course, glorious leader." Porter said grandly.

"You know I fucking hate that."

"Oh, too fucking bad for you. I like it."

"Yes, I guessed as much."

"Mason," James said from the other side of the table, "How did it go?"

"They wrapped him up like a lovely Christmas present and bundled him off with no trouble."

"There's a gift with no return." Juan smiled. "A toast to getting rid of him!"

They all drank.

Porter looked a bit puzzled still. "Who was he trying to hit, though? Senator Ford never approached me or talked to me, and I never snubbed him that I know of, although I certainly may have without knowing it."

"Me." James said quietly. "I told him to get lost when he tried to order a piece from me and wouldn't pay for it. He seemed to think he was doing me a favor and would pay me in status and exposure."

Porter nodded. "I rather thought so."

"I don't need him to make or break me."

"No, you fucking don't. You can make or break yourself."

Michael grinned. "Although I think Callie might have something to say in that department."

Callie blushed. Everyone else clapped and cheered. Mason let the conversation around him wash over him like the golden light of the study itself. He felt at peace with the world and with himself again. They had pulled a mean man out of office and taken the poison out of him. Perhaps things would calm down a bit for a while now.

Or, perhaps not. The Secretary still had his phone number, he still had his clearance, and the world was still fucked up.

Either way, Mason had a group of people he trusted beyond anyone else in the world, and they could fucking take anything that was thrown at them, no matter what.

Bring it, world, he thought as he accepted his cards from Porter. He tossed in his chips.

www.ingramcontent.com/pod-product-compliance
Lightning Source LLC
Chambersburg PA
CBHW050855150626
46549CB00013B/1894